RED ROCK

Kate Kelly

First published in 2014 by Curious Fox,
an imprint of Capstone Global Library Limited,
7 Pilgrim Street, London, EC4V 6LB – Registered company number:
6695582

www.curious-fox.com

Cover design by Steven Mead
Cover illustration by Rhett Podersoo courtesy of Advocate Art

ISBN 978 1 78202 061 5
17 16 15 14 13
10 9 8 7 6 5 4 3 2 1

A CIP catalogue for this book is available from the British Library.

Typeset in Palatino 10.5 pt

For Alex and Eileen, with love.

1
Gunshots

I'm not sure why I looked towards the window at that moment. Maybe a movement caught my eye. I don't really remember what with everything that followed. I put down my phone and, as I turned, the security light blinked on. A pool of yellow flashed across the lawn in the twilight. Then something moved in the gloom beyond.

I froze, staring hard at a patch of deeper shade amongst the shrubs at the bottom of the garden. The rain had stopped and the dusk was closing in fast. The shadow moved again and I held my breath. A human figure.

I almost felt a click as his eyes met mine. He was looking right at me.

"Uncle Robert!" I yelled, and sprinted down the corridor towards the kitchen.

"Uncle Robert!"

I burst into the kitchen. Robert looked round, up to his

elbows in rubber gloves and dirty dishes.

"What's up, Danni?"

"There's someone in the garden." I gasped for breath.

Robert peeled off the gloves and dropped them onto the draining board. "Maybe we'd both better take a look." He winked at me as if to say: *I bet you're imagining things.*

I kicked off my slippers and slid my feet into my wellies. Robert reached for the shotgun as I wound our torches.

"So did you really see someone or is this a ploy to get me away from the housework?" His tone was light but he was loading that shotgun.

I handed him his torch. "I really saw someone."

He nodded and opened the back door. A blast of cold air made me shiver. Summer evenings had once been warm. At least, that's what people said. No time now to go back for a coat.

"Where did you see him?" Robert panned his torch beam across the base of the wind turbine, shining the light along the barrel of his gun.

"Over here." I directed my torch at the bushes. The leaves glistened with the recent rain, and in the beam the shadows vanished. Robert lowered his gun and wandered over for a closer look, scanning the ground.

"Looks like you were right."

The grass squelched beneath my feet as I joined him. The lawn was mainly moss these days, the garden reverting to marsh. Robert passed his light over the ground, and there, between the bushes and the fence, was a footprint. I leaned forwards for a better look.

"What do you think he was doing?"

"Well, it looks like he came in over the fence here." Robert moved the beam of light up from the ground to shine it out across the field beyond. It was getting darker and I squinted into the gloom. But apart from a couple of rabbits dazzled by the light there was nothing to be seen; just the darker shadows of the hedgerows and, beyond, the ever-expanding estuary.

"Burglar?" I suggested. I didn't want to say "scavver". *Don't think about it. Don't think that they might have come this far.*

Robert nodded. "Most likely checking things out. Let's hope we've put him off." He squatted down to study the footprint once more. He looked so serious crouching there.

"Uncle Robert, the great tracker," I said and tried not to giggle.

He glanced up at me. "You can tell a lot from someone's footprints, you know."

"Really?" I peered down over his shoulder.

Robert shrugged and stood up. "Well, some people can."

I laughed. "I bet you could if they were a thousand years old."

"But that's archaeology. That's different. Not like these modern footprints. They're jumbled and meaningless. A bit like that music you like." He winked at me.

I pretended to gasp. "You can talk. What about that hideous music you and Mum are always..."

I swallowed.

Mum.

Robert went back to panning his torch beam around the bushes. I stared past him, out over the fields and towards the estuary. The first bats of the evening flitted against the grey of the sky.

Robert sighed and I could see him looking at me in the darkness. "Look, Danni. I know it can't be much fun having to spend the summer here with me. But it's not that bad really. I grew up here. We had a great time."

I tried to smile. I could feel that familiar tightening in my throat. "I'm not complaining. Just a bit lonely, I guess."

Robert nodded. "I miss your mum, too. She was the best big sister in the world."

I didn't answer. I stared at the pool of torchlight, at the grasses and the drops of water that reflected the light. I stared at anything other than Robert and swallowed hard. *Please don't talk about Mum and Dad.* After a while, I heard him draw in a deep breath.

"Tell you what, Danni," he said. "Maybe I can make some time for you after all." I looked up at him. "Shall I see if I can arrange for us to spend a few weeks out at..."

But he never finished the question. He paused, turning back towards the house. I hardly dared breathe. He had been about to invite me to Greenland, hadn't he? Surely he had? After all, I'd been dropping enough hints ever since I got here. Why didn't he finish so I could say "yes".

There was a faint humming noise coming from the front of the house, swelling in the damp air. For a moment I couldn't make out what it was. Then I heard the crunch of gravel beneath wheels and it clicked.

"That's a lekkie car," I said, and my pulse quickened. "Someone's coming up the drive."

Robert nodded. He started to march back across the lawn and I squelched after him. We rounded the side of the house, sodden lawn giving way to crunchy gravel path. Who could be coming here at this time of night? The roads weren't safe

8

after dark. Everyone knew that.

The porch light was on and a small electric car had pulled up on the drive.

As I moved forwards, the driver climbed out; she was a slight woman, her fair hair scraped back into a ponytail, wearing faded jeans and an over-large jumper.

My heart jumped. The Mars Mission only returned the day before and my aunt Kris wasn't due back here for another two weeks.

"Kris," I shouted, running now.

She saw me and smiled, then started towards us, arms out in welcome.

"Kris?" said Robert, and I could hear the break in his voice. It had been so long since we had been together, with only the video uplink for contact over the past two years. Kris's smile widened into a laugh as she reached out to us.

But then she faltered.

Something changed in her eyes, a look of surprise, and then fear, and in that moment a loud crack sounded. I flinched as if someone had punched me. Kris dropped to her knees. She reached to her chest and looked down at her hand. In the yellow glow of the porch light I saw that her fingers were glistening wet. She looked back up at us, pleading, and the wet was black blood that soaked and spread across her jumper.

She fell forwards onto the gravel.

I was running with a scream in my throat.

"Danni!" shouted Robert behind me. "Get down."

I paid no attention. I reached Kris and tugged on her shoulder, rolling her over. Blood spurted from her wound onto my hands and her eyes flickered open.

"Danni?" Her voice was faint, breathy, her eyes unfocused.

"Kris, Kris," I sobbed. I could barely speak.

Another shot sounded. Over by the wall of the house, a spray of gravel flew up against the windows. I ducked, and my face was close to Kris's, her breath warm on my cheek.

"Danni," she breathed. I pressed my head closer to hear. "Tell no one."

She reached for my hand, pushing her fingers between my own. There was something hard there, thrust into my palm. Then her hand fell away.

Footsteps sounded, running down the lane, fading into the night. A single shot rang out in the dark, but this time it was Robert, firing after the fleeing figure.

He was beside me now. He dropped the gun onto the ground and took Kris in his arms.

Her head fell back and her eyelids fluttered. Her eyes, once full of fire, emptied of light.

"No," screamed Robert and he pulled her close. "Kris! No." One final breath rattled in her throat. Then all was still.

"Oh, Kris," wept Robert. I squatted back on my heels and started to shake. I stared at my aunt's body cradled in her brother's arms and I was numb. I tightened my fist around whatever it was that Kris had given me in that dying moment. The tears started to roll down my cheeks.

I won't tell anyone Kris, I promise.

2

MEKA

I tucked my feet underneath me and stared numbly into the fire. Uncle Robert, standing behind me, gave my shoulder a gentle squeeze.

"Will that be all for now, Inspector?" he asked.

The policeman nodded and put his notebook away. "Once Scene of Crime have cleared up, we'll leave you alone. We'll be keeping a close eye, although I doubt they'll be back."

"So do you think it was scavvers then?" Robert asked. His voice was edgy. I reached up and touched his hand. None of this felt real.

The inspector shrugged. "Scavengers? I guess so. They don't usually come this far from the cities, but as the waters keep rising they're going to come further. There are a few things that puzzle me, though."

"Like the fact that scavvers don't usually shoot people," I suggested. I hoped I wasn't speaking out of turn.

The inspector tried to give me a reassuring smile but it wasn't very convincing. He had plump cheeks that should have been full of laughter beneath serious eyes. Maybe things were worse in the cities than I realised.

"It's fairly common for scavengers to carry guns these days," he said. "It's pretty chaotic in some of the flooded areas."

"But this was more like a sniper," I insisted. My eyes stung with tears.

The inspector shook his head. "It's worrying, I'll agree."

A log spat a shower of sparks into the chimney and the fire flared for a moment. A shadow moved in the doorway.

"Inspector."

I looked round. A large figure loomed: a man in a suit who had greased-back hair and shoes so highly polished that the firelight reflected off them.

He marched up to the inspector and flashed an ID card.

"Morgan Pew," he said and snapped the card shut.

"The Mars Exploration Agency?" said the inspector scowling at the patch of empty air where the card had been. "What interest does MEXA have here?"

Pew didn't reply at once. He turned, surveying the room, his grey eyes lingering first on Robert and then on me. I curled myself up as small as I could.

"Kris Quinton was an employee of ours," he said. "And now I would like to ask these people a couple of questions." He smiled at me, but there was darkness in his eyes.

The inspector squared his shoulders.

"Well, really, this is not…"

"Thank you," said Pew, curtly. "But I would like to like speak to them alone."

"As the inspector in charge of this case…"

Pew turned round to face him, an edge of steel in his tone. "Please leave us."

The inspector stared at him. The corner of his mouth twitched and I could see the fight in him shrivel under Pew's glare.

Pew smiled. "Thank you, Inspector."

The inspector gave an indignant snort and marched from the room, muttering under his breath. Pew turned back to me and Robert, his lips drawn back from his teeth. It was more of a snarl than a smile.

The fire had started to die down and a chill was creeping into my skin. Robert added another log, then sat down opposite me. Pew took up the inspector's position in front of the hearth, holding his hands out behind him towards the flames, blocking the heat from the rest of us.

"How can we help?" Robert asked. He looked tired, black circles under his eyes. The light of the dying fire flickered across his face.

"First, I am so very sorry about what has happened to Kris," Pew began. "She was a wonderful person and we're all going to miss her terribly." I bristled at his words. They sounded almost too sincere, rehearsed. I thrust my hands deep into the pockets of my fleece, and my fingers touched on the object that Kris had given to me as she died. *Tell no one.* I still hadn't had a chance to look at it.

Pew pulled a packet of cigarettes from his pocket. "Do you mind?"

"Well, actually…" Robert began, but Pew was lighting one without waiting for an answer. Robert and I exchanged glances.

"Can you tell me if she said anything to either of you before she died?" Pew asked. He was still smiling, but something in the tone of his voice had hardened.

I tightened my fingers around the sharp, jagged object in my pocket.

"No," I said, struggling to keep my voice even. "She never had the chance."

"I heard her say 'Danni'," said Robert. I froze, trying not to show any reaction, but my heart was pounding.

"And you're quite sure she didn't say anything else?" Pew pressed, giving me a hard stare. Smoke trickled out between his teeth and drifted in thin tendrils across the room.

"Quite sure," said Robert. I nodded in agreement.

"Hmm." Pew rubbed his chin and looked around at the pictures on the walls, the photographs and Robert's archaeology finds on the mantelpiece.

He picked up one of Robert's rock specimens and turned it over in his hand.

"And did either of you remove any objects or personal effects from Kris or her car?"

"No, of course not," said Robert. I could tell by the way he was sitting forwards that the questions were starting to irritate him.

"Your rock collection?" Pew asked, holding Robert's rock up in front of him and squinting at it.

"Yes."

"An interesting specimen." He weighed it in his hand. "Strangely light."

Robert didn't answer.

"Interesting markings. Almost like writing. Where did it come from?"

"Greenland." Robert reached out towards Pew for the rock, but Pew pulled it away.

"Ah yes, you're the archaeologist, aren't you." It wasn't a question. His eyes narrowed and he slipped the rock into his pocket. "I might just keep this, if you don't mind."

"It's just a lump of rock." Robert sat forward, rigid.

"So, are there any more interesting specimens around here?" He gave Robert a probing stare.

"No."

"No?" Pew raised one eyebrow. "Well, perhaps I should take a little look around, since I'm here."

"I don't think so."

Pew cracked his knuckles, one at a time. "It won't take me long."

"Not without a warrant." Robert's jaw was set firm as he spoke. The atmosphere prickled with tension.

"I can have this place turned over, you know. My men are outside. I just need to snap my fingers." Pew raised his hand, miming the gesture.

"And so are the police. MEXA may be many things, but you're not above the law."

Pew lowered his hand.

"I don't know what you mean."

"Yes, you do. Everyone knows that you're more than just a space agency."

"In which case a few local constables would hardly be a problem."

"But the press would be. It's hardly going to reflect well on MEXA if you're ransacking my house when they get here."

Pew paused. A muscle twitched in the corner of his eye. Then he turned back towards the mantelpiece.

"A warrant can be arranged."

He picked up one of the photographs. "You and Kris, I presume?"

Robert nodded. It was the picture of them as kids, riding donkeys on a beach, back when the summers were warm. There weren't many beaches left these days. Not nice sandy ones like that.

"And the third person? Another sister?"

Robert nodded.

"My mother," I said, and my voice caught in my throat.

Pew gave a soft grunt and put the picture back.

"Ah yes, of course. You look just like her. A tragic accident. Drowning, wasn't it? So sad, to lose both parents like that."

How dare he! I clenched my fists inside my pockets, trying not to let my anger show.

"What do you want from us?" I said, my voice cracking. He didn't look around. He ran his fingers over the frame and continued staring at the picture.

"Danni," Robert was rising to his feet.

But I wasn't listening. "Why can't you leave us alone?"

And then it was all too much. Kris dying in Robert's arms, and now this man. My feet were on the ground. I wanted to scream. I wanted to hit him.

I turned and fled from the room.

"Danni!" Robert shouted, but the sound of his voice was smothered by the blood rushing in my head. I ran. Away from Pew, away from his questions, away from those memories of pain and loss. If only they'd never gone on that diving trip – then they would still be here.

I slammed my way into the bathroom, the room cold with evening chill. I leaned on the sink and deep breaths caught as sobs in my throat. My reflection stared back at me, puffy red eyes and tear-streaked cheeks. I parted my lips and sucked in the cold air. *Why did Pew have to mention Mum and Dad?*

And then I remembered, deep in my pocket, the thing that Kris had pressed into my hand as she died. I dug it out and studied it as it lay on my palm. It looked as if it was made of stone, but at the same time it didn't look natural.

The blood on it had dried and formed brown flakes that stuck to my pocket fluff. I thrust on the tap and watched the water run over it, a dark stain swirling into the sink, red against the white. I rubbed at it with my thumb and it started to come clean.

There were strange markings on it. Odd lines etched into its surface that I could see only when it caught the light at a particular angle.

"Danni!"

I jumped at the sound of Robert's voice and a rap on the bathroom door. I shoved the object back into my pocket.

"Danni, are you all right?"

I eased the door open and looked up at Robert.

"He's gone," he said. "They've all gone."

I let out a long slow breath and opened the door wider.

"Good."

Robert paused. He looked like he was making his mind up about something.

"Pack your bags, Danni. We're leaving."

"What? Now?"

Robert gave me a rueful smile. "No, it's too dangerous to travel by night. But first thing in the morning. We're not staying here. Not with this happening so soon after your parents... We're going to the dig site."

"But Pew..."

"Pew will be back in the morning, with his warrant. He won't be able to get one tonight."

"Won't he guess that's where we've gone?" I wiped my hands on my jeans. They felt clammy and cold.

Robert was looking at me, his eyes intense. "Maybe, but I have to go there. We're on the brink of something really special. I can't afford to miss it."

"Why does he want to search the house?" My heart was beating so hard I could hardly breathe.

Robert glanced behind him, as if he feared someone might be listening.

"I've got papers and stuff, up in my study. Pew mustn't get his hands on them."

"Is that what he's looking for? Is that why he wants the warrant? To search the house for your stuff?"

"Yes. I think so."

"But why?"

Robert paused a moment before answering.

"Let's just say there's more to my work that just archaeology." He reached out and placed his hand on my shoulder. "Try to get some sleep."

When he had gone, I stood alone in the glare of the electric light. Kris's loss was a physical pain that wouldn't shift. But above that, pressing down, was a terrible sense of unease. There was something so wrong about that man Pew, the way he had taken Robert's rock, that rock with the strange lines on it.

I unclenched my hand and looked down at Kris's stone.

Robert's rock – that was where I'd seen those markings before.

3

Greenland

Robert woke me before dawn.

I shoved an extra T-shirt into my bag and stared around at my room. Was there anything else I'd forgotten? Which of my hats should I take? I paused for a moment, then packed two and put on my favourite – a purple velvet beret with a huge ostrich feather that swept from front to back in a wide curve.

The picture on my desk caught my eye. It was a picture taken at Christmas two years before, when we had all last been together, before Kris had set off for Mars.

I ran my fingers across the faces of my parents. Dad was kissing Mum on the cheek and she was pretending to push him away. Kris was laughing and Robert had his arm around her, and my best friend Isaac and I were doing the ugly face competition and wearing party hats. Only Lucy, Robert's soon to be ex-girlfriend, wasn't smiling.

"Are you ready?" Robert called.

I slipped the picture into my pocket.

"Coming," I called back. I looked round once more. I hadn't wanted to come here at first, but now I didn't want to leave. Too many memories left behind.

The postcard my parents had sent before they died was propped against my mirror, a rocky island and an old church on the front and a scribbled, cheerful message from my mother on the back. The newspaper cutting I had kept of Kris and her fellow astronauts as they left for Mars lay nearby, yellow and faded.

It was strange to think that they were all gone.

"Danni!"

I picked up the postcard and hurried out. Robert was waiting for me at the bottom of the stairs. He chuckled when he saw me.

"What's that on your head?"

I reached up and touched the soft velvet. "It's my new hat. The one Isaac gave me on the last day of term."

"What's with the feather?" Robert asked.

"It's a cool feather."

"That's a really mad hat," said Robert as he ushered me into the grey, pre-dawn drizzle.

There was a black car parked in the driveway, two figures slumped in their seats.

Robert laughed at my startled expression. "Special coffee. They're going to have awfully sore heads when they wake up."

I was staring at him now. Was this really my Uncle Robert? In just a few short hours he seemed to have changed.

"Are they Pew's men?"

"Yes. Now hurry, the car's over here."

I gave the two sleeping men one last glance, then hurried after Robert.

I sat yawning throughout the short drive to the airport. The roads were quiet this early, most of the world asleep, and only the distant lights of the terminal building glowed orange in the gloom as we approached. I finished a text to Isaac about Kris and pressed send. I'd call him from Greenland.

Our tickets were waiting for us. We filed through passport control and waited in line for our bags to be searched and our ID cards to be scanned. I glanced up at Robert, at his hollow cheeks and sunken eyes. And I thought I felt tired – Robert looked as if he hadn't slept in months. He must have sensed me staring.

"Are you all right? You've not changed your mind, have you?"

I tried to smile. "We left so suddenly. What about Kris?"

Robert nodded. "We'll come back to sort that. But nothing's going to happen for a couple of weeks. MEXA took her body. I've no idea when they're going to release it."

My mouth dropped open. "You didn't say… When…?"

"After you ran out. Pew pulled rank on the police. The inspector wasn't pleased." He handed over our ID cards to be scanned and I hoisted my bag onto the conveyor belt.

"I bet he wasn't. But how can MEXA do that sort of thing? I thought they were just in charge of the space programme."

The terminal lights flickered and nearly died. Robert looked up at them. The last thing we needed now was another power cut. They had been happening more and more frequently.

The power didn't fail. The lights came back on and Robert

breathed an audible sigh of relief. But we had to wait as they re-booted the X-ray machine.

"MEXA?" I prompted. "What did you mean when you said to Pew that MEXA were more than just a space agency?"

"MEXA have a lot more clout than most people realise," Robert explained, his head close to mine so his voice wouldn't carry. "They pretend to just be a space exploration programme and, of course, that's how they started out. They launched satellites into space, developed some of the cheapest and most efficient methods for doing so and pretty much cornered the telecommunications market. Then they were going to build a base on the Moon, before they switched their attention to Mars. That is the MEXA most people see. But what most people don't know is that they've got influence with all the major European governments."

"What do you mean?"

Robert lowered his voice further. "Many of the governments are in danger of losing control, especially in the countries worst hit by the rising seas. It started to get really bad about fifteen years ago when the sea defences failed and many of the coastal cities were abandoned. The worst affected countries went into financial meltdown. It was a time of political turmoil and MEXA saw the opportunity to take control, stepping in and bailing them out, taking over governments by the back door. MEXA virtually run Europe these days. They just don't care to admit to it. They present themselves as a space agency. Pull the wool over everyone's eyes – but their real ambition is power."

"Kris worked for MEXA?" I said as the conveyor belt started moving again.

"Yes, she did." He sighed. "That was my idea. I wish I'd

never suggested it."

I shivered. "What do you mean? You're talking as if MEXA killed her!"

Robert gave me a sad stare. "I don't know, Danni. I wish I did. MEXA are bad news. There's rumours they have links to organised crime and that's how they got to be so powerful. Of course, nobody can prove anything."

"And Pew?"

"Yes, that man Pew – he pretty much runs the show. He's the driving force behind MEXA. It must be important to them, if he showed up at our door." Robert smiled. "I managed to put him off for a bit last night. You can be sure he'll be taking the house apart this morning. Luckily, he won't find anything. Everything's safe in here." He patted his case. "Anyway, no point in hanging around waiting for the police to tell us we have to stay put."

"You didn't tell the inspector we were leaving?"

Robert winked at me. " 'Course not. He might have tried to stop us."

"But won't he still need to question us?" I picked up my bag as it emerged from the scanner.

"I'm sure he will. But it'll have to wait. We're needed in Greenland anyway."

"We are?"

"The dig called while you were asleep. They've got the results in from the geophysics survey. They think they've found something."

I followed him through to departures, my mind overflowing with questions. "Why did that man Pew steal your rock?"

"Yes, that piece of rock..." Robert's eyes were so serious as he said this, as if a shadow **had fallen** across his face.

The loudspeaker announced **that** our flight was boarding, and Robert shook off his frown and smiled.

"You're going to love the dig site, Danni," he said as we followed the other passengers out across the runway in the thin dawn light.

We changed flights in Iceland, boarding a small light aircraft. With my nose to the window, I watched as the plane swept low over a rippling sea. I tried to doze, but I always woke with the echo of gunshot in my ears.

Before long, Robert pointed out the coastline and I pressed my face against the glass, peering at the scene below.

Greenland.

Only it wasn't very green. It was more a montage of greys and browns, miles and miles of it, all looking the same. Of course, thirty years ago it would have been white, a vast expanse of ice, now melted and discharged into the oceans.

"The glaciers once came all the way to the coast," Robert said, as if he had been reading my thoughts. I stared down and tried to imagine this whole landscape covered with ice.

"What was it like, watching it change?" I asked.

"Scary, at first." He sat back in his seat. "At first they weren't sure whether the seas were actually rising or it was just that the weather was more severe. But then the ice started retreating faster than anyone had predicted. The coastal areas began to flood. The waters are still rising. Nobody really knows how much further."

"I suppose we've learned to live with it." My breath was steaming up the window and I wiped it clear with my sleeve.

"I miss the warm summers, though," said Robert. He was staring blankly at the seat in front of him. I knew he was missing more than just the summers. He was missing the people he had shared those summers with – my mum, and Kris.

I bit my lip to stop the tears. I missed them, too.

"There's the camp," said Robert at last, as the pilot lined us up with a landing strip, a flat brown rectangle amid the uneven terrain. To the side of it were white and grey patches of tents and awnings. It looked tiny from up here.

The aircraft banked and dropped. It bounced onto the ground and taxied round to stop near the tents, engine whining and prop spinning. The pilot climbed out of his seat and lowered a small set of steps.

"Here you go," he said, and gave me a wink. I followed Robert down into the sunshine.

Two of the people from the tents had come over to greet us. One of them handed a bundle of post to the pilot, who gave a wave of his hand before closing the door. I watched as the aircraft jolted away across the stony runway.

"This is my niece, Danni," said Robert. The two men smiled in greeting.

"Welcome to Greenland," said one.

"Hope you don't mind roughing it," said the other, grinning. Neither looked as if they had washed or shaved in weeks.

Robert put his hand on my shoulder. "Simon and Doug. Come on, Danni, I'll show you around." He started to lead me towards the tents.

"When do you want to meet the new girl?" asked Doug.

Robert stopped and scowled at him. "What new girl?"

"Flew in last night. Someone's daughter on a work placement." Simon scratched at his gut, which was spilling out over the top of his jeans.

"And the geophysics results are in," said Doug. "There are some interesting anomalies up towards the ice front."

"Really? That close?"

Simon nodded. "I think this is it, Rob. I think we've found it."

"Excellent. I want to see those." Robert's eyes were sparkling. "I'll meet you in the main tent in a few minutes." He threw my bag over his shoulder.

"Come on, Danni. This way." He started off once more towards the clustered tents and pointed to one on the edge of the camp. "That's my tent, and I've had the team set yours up just over here."

It was a tiny two-man tent set aside from everyone else, sheltered by a large boulder. A bright blue dome of canvas, snuggled amongst the browns and greys of the landscape.

"Your suite, my dear." He unzipped it and held open the flap for me to look inside. There was a sleeping bag and a couple of books beside a wind-up lantern. I turned to him and smiled.

"Thanks."

Robert grinned. "What for?"

"For bringing me here, to Greenland, to a real archaeological dig. For my fabulous tent."

"It's not very big."

"It's the best hotel I've ever stayed in."

Robert threw back his head and laughed. He hadn't laughed since Kris... I reached up to touch the thing she had given me, now tied with black cord around my neck and tucked away under my T-shirt. I'd kept my promise. I hadn't told a soul.

"Say that again when you haven't washed for a week and you're dusty and dirty and your hair..." Robert began.

"I won't mind."

He tipped his head to one side, looking at me.

"Will you be okay here?" he said. "I've got to go and check out this geophysics data."

I nodded.

"Good. Feel free to walk round and ask questions, but don't go wandering off."

I waited until he had gone and then I zipped up my tent.

Don't go wandering off.

I could hear the echo of his voice in my head.

Don't go wandering off.

It was a lovely sunny day. How could a little bit of wandering possibly hurt?

4

The Ice Front

I looked around the dig site. The valley was barren, filled with random piles of gravel and loose stone. Only the runway formed a smooth path through it. The tents were clustered around the edges of the camp and in the middle was a series of large awnings and a bigger tent, more like a marquee, which I guessed was where the archaeologists gathered to eat and work on their finds. I could hear the tinny sound of a pop song on the radio and a deep male voice coming in for the chorus. Simon or Doug, probably.

I pulled my phone out of my pocket as I walked and watched the screen power into life. I couldn't wait to tell Isaac where I was. But my phone had other ideas: the words 'No Signal' flashed at me across the screen. I shoved it back into my pocket. Now that I couldn't call him, I wanted to more than ever.

We'd always spent the holidays together, ever since I'd

known him. Last summer we'd gone to a sailing camp out on the Italian lakes. I smiled at the memory, even though something ached inside me at the same time.

There was a stream running through the middle of the valley and that was where I went first, following the sound of the water bubbling over the rocks. I sat down on a large boulder that jutted out into its path, half damming it, and the water swept round in a tight arc carving a deep gully.

The water was blue and slightly opaque and, when I reached out to touch it, icy cold. I let it run over my fingers until they had lost all feeling and then I pulled my hand away. My fingers ached as the blood returned. First my parents, then Kris. I only had Robert now in the whole world. And Isaac, of course, but Isaac wasn't family. Isaac wasn't *here*, and I couldn't even phone him.

"Glacial melt water," said a voice behind me, making me jump. I looked around, blinking up at the figure silhouetted against the brilliance of the sky.

"Hi, I'm Gracie." The figure climbed down onto the rock beside me. She was the last thing I expected to see in the middle of nowhere. She looked about eighteen or nineteen, her hair dyed black and tied up in an edgy style and a touch of glitter around her eyes. Even her clothes and boots looked too trendy for a dig site. I suddenly felt very scruffy and dirty, and I'd only just arrived.

"I like your hat. Cool feather." She held out a packet of gum towards me. "Do you want some?"

I took a piece. "Thanks."

"I heard you were coming." She gave a flash of perfect white teeth. "You're Danni, aren't you?"

I nodded.

"I'm glad you're here. Now I'm not the only girl on the dig."

There was something so welcoming about her; her friendliness was disarming. I couldn't help smiling.

"Have you been here long?" I asked.

Gracie shook her head. "No. I only got in last night."

"Are you the new placement student the others were talking about?"

"Were they?" Gracie's cheeks flushed. "I guess that'll be me."

"So, aren't you supposed to be digging?" I looked at the row of buckles on her boots. She didn't look like an archaeologist.

Gracie laughed. "No. My dad said I should come out here and get some work experience. He decided that the great outdoors would do me good after spending the last few months swotting for exams."

"Is this what you want to do, then?" I asked, gesturing towards the cluster of tents. "Archaeology?"

Gracie giggled and gnawed on the side of her cheek. "I don't really know what I want to do," she said. "I'd like to take a gap year and go travelling, but my dad isn't too keen. He says it's either university or go and work for him." She pulled a face. "I can't think of anything more boring."

"Archaeologists get to go to all sorts of interesting places. Just look where we are now." I rubbed my hand over the rock I was sitting on. It was smooth, scoured by millennia of ice erosion.

Gracie looked around. "Hmm, yes. A barren landscape, rock and dirt. No plants, no animals. Bit of a dump, really."

I laughed. "I guess the archaeologists don't see it that way."

She grinned at me. "Not much of a dig, though. They don't seem to have found anything."

"They're all getting rather excited over some geophysics results."

"Are they?"

"They said there was something up near the ice front."

"Really?" Gracie was staring around, shielding her eyes from the sun. "Fancy going for an explore, then?"

"The ice front? Do you know where it is?" I scrambled to my feet, trying not to look too eager.

"Yes. It's not far at all."

"Sounds like a plan," I said. I knew I shouldn't really wander off, but all of a sudden I yearned for some company. Someone to take my mind off Kris, my parents, how much I missed Isaac.

We set off up the valley, following the path of the stream. Gracie chatted about the dig and mocked the archaeologists as we clambered over boulders and scrabbled our way through piles of loose gravel. She made it all sound comical and our laughter echoed around the mountains.

"This is more fun than digging and dirt," she said with a smile as we paused to catch our breath.

Soon the camp was a good way behind us. It seemed tiny from up here, a patchwork of canvas in the middle of nowhere.

"There's the ice front." Gracie pointed to the high looming cliffs ahead. The glacier front looked brown and dirty.

"Is that it?" I said.

"If we climb up the side of the valley, we'll get a better

view. Maybe we'll be able to see whatever they've found."

"Okay. Good idea." I wasn't too bothered about the view, or what the archaeologists might have found. Maybe, on higher ground, I'd get a signal on my phone.

Gracie was surprisingly agile and I had to work hard to keep up with her. There were big heaps of gravel, quite high up the valley sides, and they made for heavy going. By the time Gracie stopped, I was breathing hard.

"There," she said. "Take a look at that. This glacier is retreating faster than ever. We're probably going to be the last people to look at this ice cap. A couple more years and it will all be gone."

I glanced up from my still signal-less phone and followed her gaze. It was an incredible sight: the high ice cliffs and the water rushing out from its base.

"Wow, Gracie…" I started to say.

But then my voice was whipped from me. My foot slipped and the ground vanished. I was sliding, falling in a flurry of loose stone into darkness.

5
The Cavern

I screamed as the darkness closed around me. There was emptiness below and emptiness above and air rushing past. I had a sickening feeling that these were my last moments on Earth.

Then I was sliding among loose stones. When I came to a halt I lay still as a few stones slipped past me and finally stopped. Above, the patch of skylight was pure and clear. I could just make out the silhouette of a head peering down at me from about five metres up.

"Danni?" Gracie called. "Are you hurt?"

I sat up and looked around. There was nothing but blackness. Only the patch of light and Gracie's head above.

"I'm fine," I shouted up to her. My voice echoed and I turned my head at the noise. It sounded like I was in some sort of cavern.

"I'll go and get help," Gracie called.

"No, don't."

Robert didn't need to know about this. If I could just get out. I'd only been here an hour and I'd disobeyed him already. I didn't want to give him an excuse to send me away.

I fumbled in my pocket for my lucky key fob and the tiny toy torch I kept attached to it. Hopefully the batteries still had some power. I twisted it on and the thin beam pierced the darkness like an orange skewer. My hat was lying close by and I grabbed it and shoved it back on. I panned the beam over the gravel slope around me. It was steeper behind, and it led almost up to the patch of light where I had fallen through. That didn't look too bad.

"I think I can climb out," I called up to Gracie, trying to sound brave. I didn't want her to think I was just a stupid kid.

I shone the beam into the empty space around me. And that was when I froze. That was when I saw it.

This wasn't a cave, carved out of the rock by the action of water and ice over millions of years – no, this was artificial. The beam of my torch could just about pick out the far wall. Nearer though, the walls were perfectly smooth, pale and reflective. It looked as if the rock had been covered with plaster.

I stood up, wobbling slightly in the dark as the stones shifted beneath my weight. Gracie's head was still there, looking down at me, and now I could see that the hole through which she looked was a perfect oval – a doorway or hatch of some kind.

This place was man-made, most definitely.

"Danni?" Gracie called again.

I moved around in the dark, taking care not to slip and

fall. I started to tingle inside.

"Gracie, you've really got to see this."

"Why, what's down there?"

"Some sort of bunker," I called.

"I can't see you," she said.

I turned and started to scramble up the gravel slope towards the light. It was heavy going since every step brought more of the rubble sliding down, but soon I could reach up and touch the lip of the opening. I climbed a bit higher and pushed my head out into the sunlight.

Gracie looked relieved.

"Come on. It's amazing." I ducked back down and half slid, half scrambled down the gravel pile. For a moment she hesitated, but then I heard the stones above me crunch as she slid down to join me.

I probed the darkness with my feeble torchlight, illuminating the smooth surface of the dome structure.

"That's a rubbish torch," said Gracie. There was a sound of fumbling, then a click, and my torch beam was swamped by hers.

We were standing to the side of a massive structure, a perfect dome. Around the perimeter were openings that looked like doorways. I guessed they must lead off to other parts of the complex. This place must have been vast.

"Wow," said Gracie, staring around. "What do you reckon this was?"

"I don't know," I said.

Gracie flashed her torch beam over the walls. "Let's take a look around."

"Aren't you going to tell the others?" I straightened my hat, watching her.

"Why should we do that?" She gave me a sly grin.

And why should we. This was our find. Anyway, I knew Robert. If I wanted to explore this place, now was my only chance. Once Robert's team started investigating, he wouldn't hear of us getting in the way.

"Give me your torch," I said.

She handed it over and, as I moved forwards, I could hear her following behind.

The first of the openings was blocked by a rock fall and the second one we tried was the same. The third one led into another, smaller chamber.

As I stepped out into it something crunched beneath my boot and I pointed the torch at the floor. I stopped dead. Staring back at me from hollow eyes was a skull.

I panned the torch beam around the skull. Bones, a skeleton, and there beneath the arm bones was another skull – a smaller one, and tiny bones.

I shivered. There'd been a child here. The mother embracing it even in death.

I shone the torch out across the floor of the chamber. The whole floor was covered with a mass of bones. Hundreds of skeletons, all piled together in the dust and dirt.

"Oh my God," Gracie breathed. "They're all dead."

"What could have done this?" I said. There were so many.

"I don't think we should go any further," said Gracie. "This needs to be properly examined."

She was right. I started to pick my way back into the tunnel, careful not to damage any of the bodies. They lay where they had fallen, their bones still in place, skulls intact.

I moved the light away and left them in darkness.

I panned the light over the scree slope that we had come down. But I wasn't ready to leave, not just yet.

"Shall we check out another one of these tunnels?"

Gracie stiffened and turned towards me. She hesitated a moment, then shook her head.

"No, we should go back – fetch the others."

"You're afraid?"

"Actually, yes."

I tried to sound reassuring. "So am I, but I still want to look. Anyway, they're dead. They can't hurt us."

I flashed the beam into her face and she lifted her hands to shield her eyes.

"All right," she said. "Just one more."

I picked the opening next to the one that held the bodies. Another tunnel led to a chamber, exactly the same size and shape, and with the same floor of human remains.

I passed the torch beam over the bodies, the skulls, the bones. There was no sign of flesh or clothes. And then I noticed something else.

There seemed to be fragments of something in a heap in the middle of the chamber.

I started out through the bones, taking care to tread between them. Hollow eye sockets stared up at me as if scolding.

"Danni, what are you doing?" Gracie whispered, her voice echoing round the chamber. She hung back in the shadow of the tunnel.

The objects were pale in the torchlight and looked like fragments of something larger. I picked one up and shone the light over it, turning it over in my hand so that one by one all its surfaces were illuminated.

It looked just like the rock Robert had kept on his mantelpiece – the rock that Pew had taken with him.

One of the surfaces was etched with a series of lines. The same odd markings that Robert's rock had. The same as the object I wore around my neck. I reached up and touched it through my jumper, pressing it against my chest. It was hot, burning into my skin. The larger fragment was heating up too and I dropped it. A small puff of bone dust rose from where it fell. *Kris? What was this?*

I turned back towards Gracie, shining my torch in her direction. The beam flickered around the walls, lighting them in a pattern of shadows and dark that seemed to move as the light passed. I picked my way closer. There were markings, strange lines – the same lines as on the fragments but deeper, more defined.

"Gracie, it's writing," I said.

She muttered something under her breath and crept out from the tunnel to join me.

"Where?"

I gestured with the torch.

She turned towards me, her eyes reflecting the light that bounced back off the walls.

"That's never writing," she said. "I've never seen anything…"

"Neither have I, but I tell you, that's some kind of writing." My heart was pounding. "What was this place?"

Gracie stared around. "Do you reckon it could be twentieth century? Some sort of military installation. You know, back during the Cold War?" Her eyes were shining, reflecting the torchlight.

"But it would have been under the ice cap. Wasn't that,

like, a kilometre thick?"

"Hmm." Gracie watched as I panned the torch beam around the walls. "Maybe being under a kilometre of ice was exactly what they wanted." There was an eager edge to her voice.

"I think it's older than that. How about Viking? The writing could be runes."

Gracie shook her head. "No chance. The Viking settlements were nearer the coast and, anyway, this whole area has been beneath the ice sheet for, like, a hundred thousand years. It's definitely not going to be Viking. They didn't have the technology to dig so deep."

"Well, what else could it be?"

"I still think it's some sort of secret military facility."

"It could be Inuit," I suggested. "Nobody else ever came here."

Gracie shook her head. "The same thing still applies. This place has been under kilometres of ice since before the first people had even left Africa." I shone the torch beam at the smooth walls and the strange script. She had a point.

"It's got to be older than last century," I said. "Look at the bodies. No clothes or flesh or anything."

Gracie stared at me. "Less than a hundred years, frozen under the ice and there'd be something left. You're right. These bodies must be much, much older. Give me the torch, I want a closer look."

She reached out to take the torch but as I handed it over it slipped from my grasp. It rolled to lie still amongst the bones, lighting one of the broken skulls from behind. It made it look as if the eye sockets were glowing, staring back at me, willing me to find the answers.

6

The Raid

Robert was leaning over one of the skeletons laid out on a lab bench in the main marquee. Now that a whole skeleton was assembled, it was clear there was something odd about it. For a start, it was small – not much bigger than me – and the face seemed slightly elongated. The skull sloped at a steep angle to bulge at the back, and the canine teeth were unnaturally large.

Robert looked round. "I can't get over this. Here we are for weeks, and we just find a few rocks. You're here less than a day, and you go and find the mother lode." He gave me a half-smile, but his eyes were worried. I pointed at the bones in front of me, at the strange skull.

"It's incredible. It isn't human, is it?"

"No, it's not."

"Is it an alien?" I asked, leaning over the skull for a closer look.

Robert rubbed his chin. "Now that really would be something."

"Is it from Mars?" I was thinking about Kris and the artefact she had pushed into my hand.

"It's not an alien," said Robert. "It's a very ancient hominid."

"A Neanderthal?" I suggested.

"Try something older."

"Older? But I thought older were apes?" I touched the end of one of the canine teeth. It was sharp.

Robert moved a jawbone into position. "This is something new to science. Maybe I should name them after you – *Homo danni*. What do you think?"

"Don't they already have a name? When we told you what we'd found, you called them the Proto People."

"That's true, but they still need a scientific Latin name." He ran his finger along one of the bones.

"And the rocks I found? They're like that piece..." I was going to say "piece that Pew took" but something made me hold my tongue. There was more to this than just a pile of old bones.

"Yes, my rock," said Robert, taking up his camera and walking round the table, lining up shots of the skeleton. "I found that further down the valley. But now we've got the whole thing, thanks to you." He pointed to the pile of papers lying on the bench beside the body. "Ten years of research to get me this far. But all I really needed was a fourteen-year-old girl. Danni, this is going to change the world."

"So this is what you've been looking for all these years?"

Robert smiled and continued taking photographs. Then he paused, looking down at the skeleton. "But why the bodies?" he muttered to himself.

"What do you mean?"

"All these bodies. We didn't expect to find all these bodies. The rocks yes, but not bodies." The camera clicked. "It's a bit odd."

Now that I was close to the fragments again I could feel the stone that Kris had given me warming up against my skin.

I prodded one of the rocks."That's writing on them, isn't it?" Robert nodded.

"Lucy could probably work out what it means," I said, smiling at him.

"Don't go there, Danni."

"Why not? I liked her."

The camera clicked again and he moved on round the table. "I liked her, too. I still do."

"I think she liked you."

"So throwing your drink over someone is a sign of affection? Hmm, the youth of today."

I laughed. She had thrown her drink over Robert and stormed out of his house that Christmas Eve, a mass of angry bouncing curls. Mum and Dad had been there, too. I touched my fingers against the photograph I had brought with me, tucked away in my pocket. The old ache was back, pulling at my insides.

I picked up two of the rock fragments, turning them over in my hands, sliding against each other, until they seemed to slot together of their own accord. A hot tingle ran through my hands and up my arms.

I dropped them and stepped back. The feeling had vanished as quickly as it had come.

"Those rocks just gave me an electric shock."

"Actually, I think I will give her a call." Robert said, ignoring me. His mind was still wandering over Lucy. "She's gone into Intelligence, MI5. Probably forgotten she ever knew anything about archaeology."

"MI5?"

Robert chuckled. "Yes. She was the best code cracker I ever knew – ancient languages were a cinch to her. She could translate Etruscan without even thinking about it."

He took a couple more shots of the skeleton and looked as if he was about to say something else when the tent flap opened and Doug poked his head around.

"Supply plane's coming," he said. "Just about to land."

Robert put down his camera. "Right on time."

I followed them out into the sunlight and down to the landing strip where I had arrived only a few days before.

The plane dropped out of the blue sky, whining like an oversized mosquito, and drew level with us. This time, the pilot killed the engine and the prop spun to a halt. He climbed down, opened the hatch and started to unload boxes of supplies. Men from the dig gathered round to help. I noticed Gracie was standing a little to one side as I moved in to do my share. She looked awfully serious.

A few trips back and forth to the marquee and the shipment was unloaded. The pilot joined us, walking between the tents towards the drifting smell of bacon.

He talked idly about the weather and the problems of the world, which all seemed so far away from us. And then he paused. "You expecting another plane?"

Robert looked round, his eyes alert. "No."

"Well, listen," said the pilot. "In fact, that's not a plane, it's a helicopter."

"And there's more than one," said Doug, smoothing his beard.

Robert's face turned a sickly grey.

"Maybe it's just some military manoeuvres," Gracie suggested. "They'll pass over."

We all turned, squinting into the sky towards the noise. My eyes started to water with the brilliance of it all, sunlight reflected off bare rock. The noise grew louder.

Then, in an instant, they were there, swooping up from behind the cliffs and filling the valley with the throb of their rotors. There were four or five, I'm not quite sure, for they seemed to be everywhere, all around us, all at once.

They dropped lower, hanging in mid-air, and I stepped back as the grit and dust of the valley floor was blasted up by the downdraft of their rotors, stinging my face. I clasped at my hat to keep it in place.

There were men now sliding down ropes to the ground, men dressed in black with heavy boots and guns slung over their shoulders. But before I closed my eyes and turned away from the driving grit, I saw something else; letters written in red on the sides of the helicopters.

MEXA.

Had they followed us here?

I blinked out the grit and lifted my hands to shield my eyes.

Simon was walking towards where the nearest commandos had just reached the ground. He was shouting, but his voice was drowned out by the throb of the rotors.

The two commandos looked at each other as he stopped in front of them, waving his arms around. I still couldn't hear what he was saying.

One of the commandos lifted his gun and took a step forward. He slammed Simon on the side of the head with it and stepped back as he crumpled into a heap. The second commando went in with a hefty kick. Simon didn't move but I could see dark blood staining his hair and the rocks around him.

Gracie screamed.

The commandos looked up. They stepped over the body and started to come towards us.

For an instant, I'm sure my heart stopped beating.

Then Robert was beside me, shouting into my ear above the thrum of the rotor blades.

"Get out of sight, Danni. Leave me to deal with this." He gave me a shove in the direction of my tent and took off towards the central marquee.

I ran. Someone was running behind me. I ducked low behind a large boulder and peered round the side. Gracie joined me seconds later.

"Why are they hurting people?" she said through ragged breaths. Suddenly, she didn't seem older and wiser than me at all.

The MEXA commandos moved in towards the archaeologists. I looked round for Robert.

The helicopters rose again and circled overhead. The sound of their rotors pulsed against my eardrums. I could see the little tent Robert's team had set up for me, hidden behind some rocks. From the rest of the camp it would be invisible.

"Come on, Gracie," I said. "I know where to hide."

She followed close on my heels as I crept around the

boulders. I paused to check that the way was clear, then darted across an open space and unzipped my tent. It wouldn't keep us safe forever, but it would buy us time. We had to get away from the camp, away from the guns, away from the MEXA agents.

Gracie scrambled in behind me, half clambering over me as I turned to peer back out.

"Can you see them?" she whispered. "Were we followed?"

"I can't see anyone. I think we're okay." I pushed my head out a little further, craning my neck to see over the boulders.

"We ought to get away from here," said Gracie. "Before they start searching the tents."

I spotted movement in the distance and drew back under the shelter of the canvas. There wasn't much room in the tent for both of us, and Gracie pressed close.

"They're after Robert's research," I told her. "I don't know why but what we found in that cavern is really important. I think that man Pew followed us here."

Gracie gave me an uneasy look. "Really?"

I held her gaze. "Yes, but he won't find everything."

For an instant a look of surprise flickered across her face. Then she stiffened.

"Danni," she whispered. "I think something moved outside."

I turned back to the half-open tent flap. At first, I couldn't see anything. But then I spotted a figure, a man, crouching behind a rock. The pilot.

"Over here!" I hissed. He flinched and jumped round, looking relieved when he saw it was only me. He crept over to join us

"Is it just the two of you?"

I nodded.

"Can you get us out of here?" Gracie asked.

"I think I can get to my plane from here," said the pilot. "Follow me and stay close."

He led the way, stooping low between the rocks.

The MEXA helicopters had landed some distance away, their rotors still, but the commandos were moving between the tents, removing things and loading them on board. I knew what they were taking.

And then I spotted Robert, his hands tied behind his back, two commandos urging him towards the helicopters with the barrels of their guns.

We reached the edge of the camp. The plane was standing on its own, not far from us.

"Fast as you can," the pilot whispered and started to run. We sprinted after him, over the stony ground. He reached the plane and yanked open the door. He didn't have time to pull down the steps but helped heave us up into the craft, almost throwing us in. Then he climbed aboard.

"Strap yourselves in," he said. My belt clicked home and the engine sparked into life. I looked out of the window as we taxied towards the runway.

MEXA commandos were running between the tents, running towards us, but they began to fall back as we picked up speed. The plane lurched and we were airborne. I let out a long slow breath. At last.

But we weren't the only ones. There was a shadow moving over the rocks below, not far behind our own. I twisted round. One of the helicopters was following us.

"Hold tight," shouted the pilot and we turned into a dive. My breath was forced from me by the movement, my heart pounding so fast that I thought my chest must burst. We veered to the opposite side, then started to climb, up, up.

"He's still there," shouted the pilot.

And then there were little puffs of cloud in the air to the side of us, and a strange staccato sound that rose above our engines and their rotors.

"Oh my God, he's firing at us!" Gracie screamed. I wanted to scream too, but I didn't have the breath. We swooped into another dive, and then we were skimming over the rocks, so low over the hilltops that I was sure we would crash. Still I didn't scream. Instead, I closed my eyes.

"Please," I whispered. "Please. I don't want to die."

Then Gracie's hand was on mine, her fingers closing around my white clenched fist. I forced a smile, which was gone almost immediately as the plane banked once more.

More shaking, more jolting. At one point, I looked down and the ground was horribly close. And then we were rising up again into the pale blue sky. But always the MEXA helicopter was close behind.

"We're going to land," called the pilot, "We're coming in steep. Hold tight."

"Where?" I asked.

"There's the an airstrip down here," he said. I could hear him on his radio, speaking to someone with an American drawl.

A moment later we hit the runway, black tarmac that shimmered in the sunlight. We bounced back into the sky and my stomach lurched up against my ribs. We bounced again, and finally slowed to a halt.

We climbed down into the sunlight. My legs were shaking and my heart was beating so hard that it made me dizzy.

A couple of angry looking men in suits were marching across the tarmac towards us, waving their arms, probably not happy about our unscheduled landing. But at least these men weren't MEXA.

At the thought, I shivered and looked up into the sky.

The helicopter had gone. Gracie reached out and took my hand, and hers was cold and clammy. I looked around into her wide eyes.

"What is this place?" she asked.

"Ruby mine," the pilot answered. "Let me do the talking."

"Are you okay, Danni?" Gracie asked.

I gave her hand a squeeze.

We were safe.

For now.

7

Heading Home

I pressed my hands between my knees and fidgeted. The cheap plastic chair wobbled. Outside, the plane was still sitting where we had landed. Gracie shifted in her seat beside me.

"How long is this going to take?" I asked. The woman had been gone with our ID cards for ages.

"I don't know," said Gracie. "Maybe there're no flights available."

"But we can't even afford to pay for a flight," I whispered.

"Don't worry about that."

I was about to ask her what she meant but she looked away, sitting upright on her chair, her toe tapping on the lino.

I checked my phone again. No signal. How could this place *not* have a phone signal?

"I hate all this sitting around. It makes me jumpy," I grumbled.

Gracie looked around. "Me too." She gave me a reassuring smile.

"I'm glad you're here," I said.

She lowered her voice to a whisper. "Back there, were you scared?"

I didn't answer. I couldn't remember if I'd been scared or not. All I could think of was the last time I'd seen Robert – with a gun to his head.

"Why did they start hitting people? And Simon – do you think they killed him?" She shifted her chair closer to mine.

I swallowed. "I don't know."

"Where do you think they took the pilot?"

"He'll be fine."

"You lost your hat."

I flinched and reached up to touch my head. I couldn't remember where I'd dropped it.

"It was a cool hat. I liked the feather."

For a few moments we sat silently.

There was a click of heels on lino and I looked up. The woman was back behind her desk.

"You're in luck. There's a routine flight going out later today. It's not the most luxurious of aircraft, but it'll get you to Iceland. You can pick up a commercial flight from there." She held out our ID cards towards us. "It's a good job you've got so much credit on your ID card." She smiled at Gracie.

I looked over at Gracie. She tucked her ID away in her pocket.

"You've got credit?"

Gracie blushed. "Birthday money. Did I tell you my Dad's quite rich?"

"No, you didn't."

"Well, he is, so there's no need for you to worry about that. I'm paying for our tickets. The most important thing is to get away from here."

"Thanks, Gracie. I promise I'll pay you back once all this is over." I looked at my phone once more, then shoved it into my pocket. The sooner we got back to England the better.

It wasn't until we landed in Keflavik that I finally got a signal.

"I can call Isaac now," I said to Gracie as we passed though security and into departures. After the tiny plane that had brought us here from the ruby mine, I was looking forward to a proper flight.

"Isaac?" asked Gracie as passport control checked her ID.

"Friend of mine."

"Friend? Boyfriend?" She winked at me.

"My best friend who happens to be a boy. He's in Italy."

"Italy? What's he doing there?" She found us a couple of seats overlooking the runway.

I dropped my bag and sat down. "Well, he lives there. He's Italian."

"Italian? Is he fit?"

I laughed. "No. He's a geek – spends most of his time on that Netgabble website. But he's the kindest person in the world."

Gracie looked disappointed. "So how do you know him? Did you meet him on Netgabble?"

"School. Boarding school. His mum's English and wanted him to go to school over here. I'm glad she did. I hated it there until I met Isaac."

Mentioning him like this, I could suddenly see him, grinning at me across the classroom from beneath a shock of dark hair. The memory was painfully vivid.

My heart pounded as I listened to the single ring tone at the other end. Just as I was about to give up on him, the line clicked and I heard his voice.

"Isaac?"

"Danni?" He sounded so pleased that my heart jumped. "Danni," he said again, but this time the tone was darker.

Gracie gestured to ask if I wanted a drink. I nodded and she wandered off.

"I'm so sorry about Kris," Isaac was saying. "I got your text, and then it was all over the news. I've been trying to call you, but your phone's been switched off and there's no answer from the house. What's going on? And where are you? You sound all echoey."

"I'm in an airport in Iceland. We're getting the next flight home." It was as much as I could do to stop myself crying. It was so good to hear his voice. I hadn't realised how much I missed him.

"You and Robert?"

"No."

For a moment there was silence. Then Isaac spoke again, fast and in hushed tones.

"Danni, what's going on?"

"The Mars Mission – MEXA." I was whispering too, cupping my hand over the phone. "I think they killed Kris." My voice started to crack.

"Why? What happened?"

"It's Robert. We were at the dig and they raided it. They took him away in a helicopter. They had guns." I swallowed back my tears. "Isaac, he's all I've got left."

"It'll be all right, Danni." His voice was gentle. "But why? Did Robert find something? In Greenland?"

I nodded, then realised he couldn't see me. "Yes," I said. "Yes, we did. Ruins and bodies, but the MEXA agents took them all."

"Did you say bodies?"

"Yes. Skeletons."

"And MEXA? What would MEXA be doing there? I thought they were just a space agency?"

"Isaac, can you do me a favour? Can you log into my email and send a message to Lucy Munroe? Tell her I'm coming to see her and it's really important."

"Danni, of course I will." He paused a moment. "Can you get here? To Italy? You'll be safe with us."

"I don't know," I sobbed. "I have to see Lucy first. I think she might know something."

"But you're all alone."

"I'm not. I'm with Gracie."

"Gracie?"

"Just another girl from the dig site."

"There were other kids on the dig?"

"No, just Gracie. She's older than me – eighteen, I think. She's doing some sort of work experience thing."

At that moment Gracie came back clutching two bottles of lemonade. The loudspeaker started to call our flight.

"I've got to go."

"Call me when you get to England."

The phone clicked and he was gone.

We followed the flow of people out onto the runway to board our aircraft. I smiled at Gracie as we strapped ourselves into our seats. She already had the duty free magazine on her knees.

"You look a lot happier," she said.

I nodded.

"So, what next?"

"Next?" I hadn't really thought past finding Lucy.

"I could help you," Gracie said. "If you like."

"But your parents? Won't they be worried?" I pulled a magazine out from the seat in front of me and started flicking through pages of adverts.

"I'll call and let them know I'm safe, but I'm in no rush to go home. There's only my dad now and he's always too busy with work."

"Maybe we should call the police when we land."

Gracie scowled. "I don't think that's a very good idea."

"Why? Do you think MEXA control the police?"

"I don't know. I just don't trust them."

"I have to find my Uncle Robert. I have to save him." I put the magazine away and turned to face her.

Gracie smiled. It was almost a patronising smile and I felt a surge of annoyance.

"I don't care what you think," I said. "There's something going on – to do with what we found in Greenland – to do with the Mars Mission. If I can find out what, it'll lead me to Robert."

Gracie was still smiling. She closed her magazine.

"And you're going to do this on your own?"

"There's more to this, Gracie. More than you know." I touched the rock under my T-shirt, pressing it into my skin, sharp and scratchy.

"What don't I know?"

"I can't tell you."

"You don't trust me?"

I shook my head. "No. It's not that. I promised."

Tears were burning behind my eyes and I blinked a few times. I wasn't going to let Gracie see me cry. Kris's words echoed in my mind – tell no one.

"So where do you start?" Gracie asked.

"Oxford."

"What's in Oxford?"

I didn't answer.

"I could help you. I mean that."

I eyed her up and down. It would be nice not to have to do this all on my own. But even so, I hesitated.

"I have credit," said Gracie.

"Why do you want to help me?"

Gracie laughed. "Because this sounds like an adventure, and I'm tired of my dad telling me what I should and shouldn't do all the time. And I'm curious. You're talking as if there's some sort of conspiracy, and some secret that MEXA don't know about."

I stared into her eyes. There was warmth there. And I was so alone. My parents, then Kris, and now Robert were gone and Isaac was so very far away. Suddenly, the thought of trying to do this alone was almost crushing. I took a deep breath.

"Okay, Gracie, you're on."

"So, what's in Oxford?"

I wasn't sure I wanted to tell her. It was a bit of a long shot, after all. But at that moment she reached out and took my hand. It felt a bit like what I imagined having a big sister would feel like.

56

"We're going to Oxford," I said. "To see an old friend of Robert's."

We caught a bus from the airport to Oxford and it dropped us off in the centre of the city. I stared around at the electric cars buzzing past, the flotillas of bicycles pulling away from the traffic lights, and wrinkled my nose at the smell of crowds of people. I wasn't used to such large places. The buildings crowded in on me.

This was a city that had changed so much, even though it was on high enough ground to avoid the relentless rising seas. Many of the lower lying districts had been demolished to make way for the levees and flood defences. The river, like most rivers these days, ran faster and deeper with all the extra rain.

In my parents' day this had been a university town, and I struggled to imagine what it must have been like with these streets full of students. Today, there were only people in sharp suits clutching umbrellas, hunched against the rain.

"Right then, how do we find this Lucy character?" asked Gracie, leaning against the bus shelter.

Good question.

"I'm not really sure."

Gracie's eyes narrowed. "I thought you said she could help us?"

"I hope she can," I said, trying to sound more sure than I felt.

"Is she with the university? Which college? Or don't you know?"

I rubbed my eyes and stifled a yawn. It had been a long couple of days.

"She was at Cambridge, but left when the flood waters came and the university shut down. She works for MI5 now."

"Ooh, MI5. What does she do there?"

"Something secret, obviously." I tapped the side of my nose. Gracie shook her head and sighed.

"So she's your uncle's ex-girlfriend, and they haven't spoken in how long?"

"A while."

"And you really think she'll help us?" She raised her eyebrows.

"Yes, of course she will. She loves him, really."

Gracie laughed and pointed along the busy street. "I think MI5 is this way."

I set off, sidestepping to avoid people coming in the opposite direction, and Gracie fell into step beside me. A diesel car drove past, a puff of smoke coming from its exhaust and I paused to watch it. You didn't see many of those these days.

My phone vibrated in my pocket as the text alert sounded. I pulled it out. Isaac. At last. I'd been trying to call him ever since we landed, but I kept being put through to his answer service. Dumb boy could never remember to charge his phone.

"We could have waited for a bus," Gracie said.

"I've had enough of buses. I'd rather walk."

I opened the text. Two words:

call me

I looked round at Gracie, and promptly bumped into an old lady who was staggering past, weighed down with bags of groceries. I mumbled an apology as she passed.

"How exactly is this Lucy going to help us? You haven't explained."

"The thing that we found in Greenland," I began. Gracie nodded and steered me into a quieter side street.

"Go on."

"Well, that strange writing that we found. Robert said Lucy might know something about it. They used to work together."

"Do MEXA know about Lucy, then?"

I shook my head. "They might, but I doubt if they think she knows anything. She was with Robert right at the start. It was when he started his trips to Greenland that they fell out and broke up."

"So they won't know we're here?"

"I hope not."

I pulled out my phone and opened Isaac's text again as we walked.

call me

MI5 was right in front of us. I'd ring him as soon I'd spoken to Lucy.

8
Inside MI5

The MI5 building was one of the old university colleges, taken over and modified after the seat of rule had been moved here from London. It still kept many of the original features, and I peered through the thick layers of bulletproof glass at the grassy quadrangle and fine stone buildings beyond.

The guard on reception wore full body armour and a hostile stare. He put down his superhero comic with a thud.

"Can I help you?" he asked in a gruff voice.

"We'd like to speak with Lucy Munroe," Gracie said, taking on the adult role. Her voice had risen a note or two.

"We don't allow anyone in without an appointment," said the guard. "Please leave quietly."

I stepped forwards, "She knows we're coming. I'm Danni Rushton. Please at least ask her."

The guard scowled at me. He checked his computer and grunted.

"Oh, yes. But it doesn't say anything about your friend."

"Please."

He looked Gracie up and down. "ID," he said at last.

I looked across at Gracie.

"Look. This is a secure building. I need ID. I can't let you through without it."

"You can wait for me here," I said. "I won't be long."

But Gracie had already handed over her ID.

I watched as he put it through the scanner. Then he moved away behind the glass screen and I could see him talking to someone on the intercom.

"Please see us," I whispered.

I had nowhere else to go.

A few moments later the guard came back. His eyes hadn't softened, and I steadied myself for rejection. But instead he nodded towards the door.

"Go on through."

Lucy was waiting for us in the corridor on the other side. She looked older than I remembered: her hair now cut short, her suit sharp and tailored, heels high, lipstick severe. She eyed Gracie up and down.

"This is my friend Gracie," I said.

Lucy smiled. "This way." She ushered us into her office. I stared around at the plush furnishings and the carved oak desk.

"Thank you for seeing us," I began as she gestured for us to sit. I lowered myself onto a leather sofa.

"It's good to see you again, Danni." Lucy perched on the edge of her desk. "I'm so sorry about Kris. I really liked her."

"Thanks," I mumbled.

"Okay then, how can I help you? Your email sounded

urgent." She glanced at her watch. "I don't have much time."

"It's Uncle Robert." I began.

Lucy's smile widened.

"Did Robert send you?"

"No." I lowered my eyes as the ache in my heart intensified. It never really went away but at moments like this, it threatened to smother me.

"Danni, what's wrong?" Despite the make-up and the smart clothes, she was the same Lucy I had known before, back before grief, before loss. I looked up at her.

"We were at Robert's dig site in Greenland. It was really amazing, and then there was a raid by MEXA agents, and they took Robert, and…"

"Wait, wait." Lucy held up her hand. "Slow down."

I took a deep breath and Lucy moved across to crouch down before me. She took hold of my hand.

"He found something, didn't he?" There was a strange intensity in those brown eyes. I glanced across at Gracie, then nodded.

"And MEXA? What did they want?"

I shook my head and the ache was crushing me again. Tears welled. Suddenly, I didn't feel very brave anymore. "I don't know. They took everything, all the finds, they took Robert."

"We only just managed to escape," said Gracie.

"I've got to find him," I said. My voice cracked as I spoke.

Lucy squeezed my hand. "I know."

"You're the only person I could think of. Before the raid he said he wanted to ask you about the writing."

"Writing?" Her eyes were blazing with interest. "You found writing?"

"Yes, it was all over the walls. And there were these strange pieces of rock and they had it on them, too."

"Do you have any of these rocks?"

"MEXA took them all."

"Oh," Lucy sighed.

The lights in the office flickered and died. Another power cut. We sat and stared at each other in semi-darkness. The disappointment on her face was still visible, even in the dim light.

Lucy gave us a reassuring smile. "The emergency generator will kick in in a minute."

I took a deep breath.

"Lucy, what do you know about all this?"

She stood up and straightened her skirt. "When we were at university, Robert was studying AE: alternative energy. He was looking into some really bizarre ideas. Energy sources that everyone said were impossible, like rain power and bovine biogas. Then he found this old thesis. It was hidden in the library, tucked away behind some old journals that nobody ever read." She glanced around, then lowered her voice. "He sat up all night reading it, over and over again, until your mother took it off him and refused to give it back until he got some sleep. I'd never seen them so excited."

"What? Mum? Did Kris know about it, too?"

"They all did. Didn't they tell you?"

I shook my head.

"That's why Robert got interested in archaeology. That's what took him to Greenland. He was looking for something – an ancient artefact that could change the world. And I think, from what you just told me, he found it."

"We found it for him, me and Gracie." I grinned at her.

Lucy smiled.

"So what was in this thesis?" I asked.

"It was a translation of some ancient texts, all about an ancient civilisation. I thought he was crazy, mind."

"Is that why you fought?"

"I suppose that was the start of it."

"So, what did it say?" I pressed.

She started pacing back and forth. "I'm afraid I don't really know. It was all rather technical and didn't make sense to me."

"But it made sense to Robert?"

"Most definitely. He seemed to think it was really important."

"Do you know where this thesis is?"

Lucy nodded, looking slightly embarrassed. "Yes. He was really worried about it falling into the wrong hands. He asked me to hide it for him and to keep where I'd hidden it secret. I thought he was being ridiculous, so I just left it on a bookshelf. Then Cambridge flooded and everyone left. It's probably still there."

"Then I'm going to find it," I said. "I have to find out why MEXA took Robert and why they want his research so much. If I can find the original texts, they might give me some answers, and maybe lead me to wherever these MEXA people are holding him." I lifted my hand to my chest, feeling the lump of the stone under my jumper. Half of me wanted to tell Lucy, but I'd made a promise and I wasn't going to break it.

"The thesis is in Cambridge and I don't think you'll want to go there. The city was abandoned ten years ago. There'll be scavvers."

"I don't care. Tell me where it is." I looked her straight in the eye. "Please."

Lucy gave me a broad grin. "You haven't changed, have you Danni?" She glanced up at the lights.

"What happened to your emergency generator?" asked Gracie.

"I don't know. It should have kicked in by now."

She tried the switch. Nothing happened.

"Maybe the fuses have blown," I said, but Lucy shook her head.

The phone started to ring.

Lucy didn't answer it. I was about to ask her why, but then the voicemail clicked in.

The guard sounded no less gruff.

"Ms Munroe? Are you there?"

Lucy looked around the office as if ill at ease. "Does anyone know you're here?"

"I don't think so."

"Well, I'm not going to take any chances." She picked up a torch from her desk and gave the handle a quick wind.

"Come with me. Now."

I stared up into her fierce eyes. I wasn't going to argue.

"Where are we going?" asked Gracie as we followed Lucy to the door.

She pulled the door open a crack and peered out into the corridor. "It's clear."

Lucy led us along the passages, her high heels clicking on the stone floors. I had to half jog to keep up with her. She kept her eyes fixed ahead. I kept glancing over at Gracie, who just shrugged.

She stopped in front of a door and switched on her torch.

"Lucy Munroe."

I looked round. The guard was waving at us from the far end of the corridor. "Ms Munroe, there are some people asking about your visitors."

"Not now," Lucy called back. She pulled the door open and ducked inside. Gracie and I followed, and the door clunked shut behind us. We were in a narrow stairwell, the light of Lucy's torch forming a yellow pool in the gloom. Lucy clattered down the stairs without a word. We followed in silence, emerging at the bottom into a large, underground car park.

I had never seen so many cars all in one place. Most were electric but there were a few old diesel models. It was by one of these that Lucy stopped.

"Can you drive?" she asked.

Gracie nodded.

"Hop in," she said. "It's open."

I took the passenger seat and Gracie climbed into the driver's side.

"Is it yours?" I asked.

"Yes." Lucy glanced back over her shoulder. "Listen, get out of here fast. You have to realise, there's more to MEXA than meets the eye."

"That's what Robert said. I think they killed Kris."

"In which case you're probably being tracked. You have to go. Now."

My mouth felt dry. "But Robert…"

She grabbed a piece of paper from her pocket and scribbled some notes. Then thrust it into my hand.

"I've written down the name of a pub. It's about fifteen kilometres east of here – go there as soon as you get the chance. There'll be some fake IDs waiting. I'll put as much credit on them as I can. Find somewhere to hole up and lie low until I contact you."

"What about the thesis?"

"I told you – Cambridge is under water and crawling with scavvers. You can't go there."

"I don't care," I said through gritted teeth. "I'm going to find it. You can't stop me."

Lucy shook her head, then took the piece of paper out of my hand and scribbled some more notes. When she handed it back to me, her eyes were stern.

"There's the thesis title and the name of the college library where I left it. It's hidden behind a copy of a book by Tacitus. At least, that's where I left it. But that was ten years ago."

Lucy was already backing away. The torchlight flickered into my eyes, dazzling me.

"I think it's a really bad idea, going to Cambridge. You're getting in over your head, just like your uncle. You should really lie low, out of sight of MEXA and let me see what I can do to help from this end."

"Thanks, Lucy."

"Go now, there's no time," Lucy said. "And don't use your real ID cards. There's some cash in the glove compartment." She started towards the stairs, then paused.

"I always cared for Robert, you know."

"When I find him you can tell him yourself," I called after her. A wave of her torch and she was gone.

"Strap yourself in," Gracie said, and started the engine. It roared into life. I'd never heard anything so noisy. Lekkie cars are so much quieter.

We lurched forwards and stalled.

"Rats," said Gracie and crunched the gears. Her eyes were wide, reflecting the dashboard lights.

"I thought you said you could drive!"

"Could you do any better?"

I didn't answer. I wasn't about to tell anyone that Isaac and I had taken his mother's car for a spin without her knowing the last time I'd stayed with him in Italy.

Isaac. I was meant to phone him.

It would have to wait.

We drove out of the car park, up a ramp and out into the street.

They were waiting for us.

Two black cars were parked across the road, armed men standing alongside. Emblazoned in red on the sides of these cars were the words MEXA.

"Oh, no!" I gasped.

Gracie crunched the gears. "Hold on tight and keep your head down."

The engine screeched as we accelerated. A voice shouted, but I could barely hear. Gracie pulled hard on the steering wheel and we lurched up onto the pavement. I saw a look of rage on the face of one of the men. He raised his gun to his shoulder, but then seemed to think better of it. He lowered his weapon and ran for the nearest car. I felt a cold chill of fear.

Then we were back on the road, speeding between rows of parked lekkie cars and bicycles propped up against walls. Pedestrians stopped and stared. I looked round over my shoulder. The MEXA agents were back in their cars and they were not very far behind.

"Can you outrun them?" I asked.

"If I can get out onto the open road. This thing seems to have a bit more power than theirs."

"So long as they don't send a helicopter," I whispered. I looked round. "They're getting closer."

The land rover lurched through a set of lights. Someone blared their horn and to the side was a screech of brakes.

We turned sharp left and jolted down narrow roads. I held on tight as I was bounced from side to side. We sped through more red lights and over junctions without stopping. But whenever I looked behind they were still there.

At last we reached an open road – a main trunk route – and the traffic cleared. Gracie put her foot down and the land rover pulled away. The agents were falling behind. I let out a slow breath.

"Are we clear?" I asked.

"I think so." Gracie eased off the accelerator and we slowed to the pace of the normal traffic: buses and lekkie cars. Faces peered out of the windows at our diesel monstrosity.

"We're a bit obvious," I said, sticking my tongue out at a boy who was staring at me. He made a rude gesture.

We turned off the main route. I pulled a map out from the side of the door and put it on the dashboard in front of me, yanking the pages open. The jolting of the land rover jerked my head back and forth and made my vision blur.

"This road is heading the right way," I said. "At least we lost MEXA."

"Don't speak too soon," said Gracie. "There's a helicopter."

I peered out and up. A dark speck was approaching from behind, drawing closer with every second. I stared at the map, but all the roads looked the same. There had to be some way out – some short cut – somewhere we could lose them.

The effort made me dizzy. This wasn't the time to get car sick.

And then I spotted something that wasn't on the map. "We'll lose him in the woods."

I pointed to the map. Gracie stared at it.

"What's this?"

"It's a map, silly."

"But what are all these weird symbols?"

I sighed. "Map symbols!"

"Oh, ha ha. How on earth do you know what it means? Nobody uses maps like this anymore."

"Archaeologists do. Turn off here." I pointed to a track heading off to the right.

We pulled off the road towards the trees. They were young trees growing on what was once arable land, now abandoned and left to return to nature. But they were big enough and they closed overhead like a green mantle.

"He can't see us now," Gracie said, looking back over her shoulder.

"I bet he can."

She glanced round at me. "But how?"

"Infra-red heat-seeking equipment." My mind was racing, panic starting to fog my thoughts. But Gracie still seemed calm.

"Then the trees won't hide us." She pulled over. "Here, show me that map."

For a few moments she pored over it. Then she stiffened.

"There. Look."

I leaned over to see what she was pointing at. The map was old – out of date – and I wasn't sure of all the symbols. But there was something.

"That's a tunnel marked there, isn't it?" she said, jabbing with her finger. "We'll hide there."

I squinted at the symbols she was pointing at. "I thought you couldn't read this thing. How do you know?"

"Because that word there says 'tunnel'." She thrust the map back into my hands and pulled away. I could see she was smirking.

We followed the woodland track for a couple of kilometres. The land rover bounced through muddy ruts and then the track vanished into an archway. Darkness closed in around us. Gracie switched on the headlamps and ahead I could see a dark tunnel vanishing into blackness.

We slowed to a halt.

"Where are we?" I asked. I could feel myself shaking.

"I think it's an old railway tunnel." Even in the pitch dark, I could hear the smile in her voice. "I don't think their heat-seeking gear will be able to find us here. At least, I *hope* it won't."

9

Scavvers

"How long do you think we ought to wait?" I asked, twisting round in my seat. My eyes had started to adjust and I could just make out pale reflections on the tunnel walls towards the entrance.

"I don't know," said Gracie. Her teeth were chattering. "Give them half an hour or so?"

"Sounds sensible."

I opened my door and climbed out, dry earth beneath my boots. I shivered at the cold air and echoing drips.

Gracie joined me, stumbling and feeling her way along the side of the land rover with her hands. She looked towards the entrance and the whites of her eyes glinted in the pale light.

"They're not going to find us," she said.

"They shouldn't." But I couldn't hide the note of doubt in my voice. I strained my ears but could only hear water dripping somewhere further along the tunnel.

"They came so fast."

"I know," I said, rubbing my arms to fend off the cold. "They must have been following us."

"Our ID?" Gracie placed her hands over her mouth. "They've been following us since we landed."

"Lucy was right, then."

"So, what are we going to do now?"

I reached up to my chest and clasped the object tight through the wool of my jumper.

"We're going to Cambridge."

"Seriously?" Gracie laughed. "Cambridge is under water. Everyone knows that. Anyway, Lucy said we shouldn't go..."

"It was only abandoned about ten years ago, when they couldn't keep the sea back any longer. Before that, well, it's where Robert and Lucy went to university. That's why the thesis is there."

"But these flooded cities – they're just not safe."

"I want answers," I said. "Anyway, nowhere's safe anymore. Not with MEXA after me."

"We need that fake ID..."

"We won't need it in Cambridge. We can get it after."

Gracie shifted her feet and shook her head. I tried to stop my teeth from chattering.

"Robert is all I have left. I have to find him. He had a secret and it's got him in trouble. The answers are in that thesis and the thesis is in Cambridge."

"Do you really think this thesis is that important?" she asked.

I folded my arms.

"You don't have to come. I'll do this myself if I have to."

"No," said Gracie. "No. I'm coming too."

She took hold of my hand in the dark. "I'm not going to let you do this alone. I understand why you have to find Robert, you know."

"You hardly even know him."

"Doug told me about your parents. What happened to them? If you don't mind me asking."

I scuffed the toe of my boot in the dirt. I did mind.

"Diving accident," I mumbled. "They were on holiday."

"Were they archaeologists, too?"

"No, they were journalists. But they went all over the world just the same."

"Cool. Did you get to go to all sorts of exciting places?"

"I wish. That's why they sent me to that horrible boarding school."

I turned away from her. I didn't want her to see the tears that were burning in my eyes. I leaned my back against the tunnel wall and let myself slide down onto the cold rough ground.

"I do understand," said Gracie. "I know what it's like to lose someone."

She came over and sat down beside me. I looked quickly round into her eyes and they were shining. Was Gracie crying?

"I had a brother," she said. "He was great, big blue eyes, mad about tractors." She was staring ahead, into the darkness, smiling at the memory.

"What happened?" I whispered. Her expression darkened.

"Leukaemia. They did everything they could. But in the end..."

I took her hand and squeezed it. "I'm sorry, Gracie."

Gracie took a deep breath. "That was when Dad changed. He always had to be in control, but this was something he couldn't stop. He hated that. Then Mum left. I remember her screaming at him. She called him a megalomaniac – said he loved power more than her. So now all I have is my dad."

"Where did your mum go?" I asked.

Gracie shivered.

"I don't know," she whispered. "She just vanished."

I didn't speak. I pressed myself close against her and I could feel her warmth.

I've no idea how long we sat in silence. I listened to the steady drip of water further down the tunnel and Gracie's soft breathing. I thought about Robert and Kris and my parents, and my heart ached.

"Do you think it's safe to head out yet?" Gracie asked eventually. It was cold here, cold and damp and I hugged myself against the chill.

"Let's take a look."

We climbed back into the land rover. Gracie fired the engine as I pored over the map. She reversed slowly out towards the tunnel entrance. Here she stopped and killed the engine, windows down. I listened hard. The air was filled with birdsong. There was no sound of a helicopter.

We jolted our way along the rutted woodland track, between tall trees and thickets of rhododendron. The woods smelled green, damp and mossy.

"We'll go across country as much as possible," Gracie said.

I ran my finger across the map, following the lines of roads and tracts of woodland.

"Sounds sensible."

"But we'll have to be careful."

She wrestled with the steering wheel as the tyres slid in the mud.

"You're worried about scavvers, aren't you?"

Gracie nodded.

"We could do without any more problems," I muttered.

After a few kilometres, she pulled over and switched off the engine."We need to stop a sec, I'm bursting."

I looked around. All I could see was green forest. "Don't go too far."

"You stay here. I won't be a minute." And with that she slipped away between the trees. I watched until she blended into the forest. Everything was still, just a few last raindrops dripping off the trees and the cawing of rooks in a nearby rookery.

I leaned back in my seat and stared up at the canopy. When I looked back down I spotted smoke, drifting up between the trees ahead of us, in the same direction that Gracie had gone. She wasn't back yet. My skin prickled as I opened my door.

I climbed down and leaf mould squelched beneath my feet. I quietly pushed the door closed and headed off in the direction I had seen her go. Whatever that smoke meant, it wasn't going to be good.

I heard them before I saw Gracie, voices drifting with the breeze. Gruff voices. Unfriendly voices. I slowed, stooping low between the branches, and crested a small rise.

There was a group of them in the road below: dirty, scruffy men with long hair and beards and dressed in rags. Scavvers. I drew in a sharp breath.

And then I saw Gracie. She was crouching in some bracken, watching them, frozen. She hadn't seen me.

The men were clustered round the burned-out wreck of a car. It was too big to be lekkie, so I guessed it had to be one of the few diesels still around, like the one we were driving. There were some bags and cases scattered across the road and three of the men were rifling through them. The other two were inspecting the remains of the vehicle.

"There's nothing here," said one of the men, tipping the contents of a case onto the road and kicking them around with muddy boots. "This was a waste of time."

"Well, they probably had their valuables on them," said another, measuring a pair of jeans up against himself. "Blame Dave for letting them get away."

He opened another case, but this time looked up and smiled. "Bingo."

The others stopped what they were doing and crowded round.

I shifted my weight, peering for a better view. What was in those cases? I took a step forwards and something snapped beneath my boot. All five men looked up at once, staring straight at me.

Cold panic clutched at my chest. I turned towards Gracie. She looked back at me from eyes wild with fear.

There was movement. The scavvers all surged forwards, running towards me, their faces crazy.

Gracie stood up, rising from the bracken.

"Run, Danni!" she shouted.

She didn't wait for me. She turned and started to sprint back through the trees, back towards the land rover. I glanced once at the men. They were pelting towards us like a pack of wolves on the scent of blood. I turned, forcing my legs to move.

The men crashed through the undergrowth behind me but my legs were sluggish – as if I was trying to run through glue. I focused my eyes on Gracie, and on the land rover ahead.

Gracie reached it first and hauled open the door, holding it for me to dive inside. As I scrambled upright she jumped in beside me. She kicked the engine into life and crunched it into gear. We lurched forwards, wheels spinning through the leaves and mud as the first of the men reached us.

He grabbed my door but I was faster, pressing down the lock. His eyes were as wild as his hair, his snarl toothless.

I grabbed hold of the door handle and bit back my screams. Gracie didn't and she shrieked in my ear. Then there was another one in front of us.

She didn't stop. She drove right at him. The one by my door ran alongside for a few seconds then fell back. The man in front stood still. I gasped as she pressed her foot down on the accelerator. He wasn't going to jump – and it was too late for us to stop.

He must have realised that in the same moment as I did and he threw himself to one side as the wheels spun past. Clods of earth and leaves and sticks were flung up in our wake.

I twisted in my seat and looked round. The man was picking himself up out of the dirt and waving his fist in our direction. Two of the others had stopped running, and the two that still came after us fell further and further behind. Soon I couldn't see them at all amongst the greens and browns.

After a while my breath slowed. Gracie pulled us off the

forest trail and onto a narrow tarmac lane, driving now at a steadier pace.

"You all right?" I asked.

"Oh, yes. This is such fun."

"They were scavvers, weren't they?"

Gracie nodded. "'Fraid so."

"I hope we're not going to meet any more like that."

Gracie looked round at me, and all trace of sarcasm had left her face.

"Unfortunately," she said, "we probably are."

10
Rising Tide

I woke, freezing cold and shivering under my thin blanket. The floor of the land rover was hard and uncomfortable, yet I snuggled up, hugging my knees to my chest. I didn't want to move.

I'd been dreaming of that Christmas, everyone together, everyone happy. I didn't want to let it go.

"Are you awake yet?"

The last threads of the dream vanished at the sound of Gracie's voice. I threw back my blanket and sat up.

The back doors of the land rover were wide open – no wonder I had felt so cold – and Gracie was outside, sitting on a log, map laid out in front of her.

"Hungry?" she asked.

"You bet." I scrambled forwards, pulled on my boots without bothering to lace them up, and joined her. She held out a couple of packets of crisps.

"Where did you get these?" I asked, taking one and ripping it open.

"They were in the back of the land rover. There's some tins and biscuits."

"Good, we'll take some food with us, just in case."

"Look what else I found." She lifted her jumper to show me a hunting knife strapped to her belt. I smiled. Very sensible. Who knew what was waiting for us in the city?

"How far to go?" I asked, shovelling crisps into my mouth as fast as I could.

Gracie waved her hand towards the fields beyond our little copse.

"I think we're close, but I still can't make much sense of this map thing."

I leaned forwards for a closer look. "I think we ought to leave the land rover here and go the rest of the way by foot."

Gracie stopped eating and stared at me.

I laughed. "Don't look so horrified. It's the safer option."

"Safe? But what about scavvers?"

"They'd hear us coming. And they'd be after our diesel. We'd never get this thing out of the city."

Gracie's mouth drooped slightly at the corners.

I folded up my empty crisp packet and looked her straight in the eye. "You really don't have to come, you know."

She crunched her crisp packet into a ball and threw it at me. "I'm not even going to answer that."

We moved the land rover into a thicket and screened it with branches and scrub until it was completely hidden from view. By the time we had finished, my arms were aching and

I was covered in bramble scratches. But unless you knew it was there, the land rover might as well not have existed.

"Follow me," I said. "And move as quietly as you can."

I led the way out of the copse, keeping to the edges of the fields. The land here was very flat, without many hedges. Quite different from the countryside where I had lived, which was all rolling hills and patchwork fields. I felt really exposed, but managed to steer us towards whatever cover there was.

A lot of the time we followed the drainage ditches, looking for places to cross. The ditches were full after all the rain. The ground was boggy and, before long, meadows gave way to marsh and the wet started to seep in through my boots.

I looked up, and ahead there were buildings rising out of the reeds.

"Cambridge." I whispered and Gracie nodded. My skin tingled.

Soon we were skirting round the back of houses. Most were deserted and boarded up. Weeds had forced their way through the patios, driveways and gardens in a tangle of growth. The roofs were green with moss, the eaves dripping with damp.

At the front of the houses was a road. Gracie crouched behind a feral privet hedge whilst I peered out, checking that the coast was clear. Derelict cars were still parked where they had been left by their owners years ago. Rust bubbled up under the paintwork and their windows were smashed. Some had the wheels removed and were propped up on bricks.

"It looks clear," I said.

I led the way, crouching low, using the cars as cover, and

darted across into another set of gardens. A broken statue stared out with empty eyes as we passed. The figure was carrying an urn that looked like it had once formed part of a water feature. We clambered through broken fences and over crumbling stone walls. More deserted roads, more overgrown gardens.

After a time, the streets grew narrow and the houses formed terraces. We lost the cover of the gardens and were forced to take to the streets.

Away from the gardens we were more exposed, and our progress slowed as we crept from one piece of cover to the next. The tarmac had given way to mud, thick and glutinous, and when I looked back, our tracks were plain for all to see.

I glanced at Gracie. She'd noticed it, too.

"Tide's out," I said. "When it comes in it'll wash our footprints away, but we'll either have to find a boat or take shelter."

"Is it far?" asked Gracie.

I swallowed back my fear.

"No, not really. We're quite near the centre of town."

Gracie moved closer for a better look at the map.

Something murmured between the walls.

"Shh," I whispered. I hardly dared breathe, every nerve on edge, senses heightened, listening. First, there was a whisper. Now there were voices.

I crouched as low as I could behind the rusting hulk of a van; Gracie pressed close beside me.

The voices were closer. I didn't want to think the word, but I couldn't help it. *Scavvers.*

Our footprints were there, bold and clear in the mud. Two sets of tracks all leading to our hiding place. They would see them. They would find us.

Gracie tipped her head towards an alleyway between the houses behind us.

I nodded.

We stooped as low as we could as we squelched between the high brick walls, wincing with every noise we made.

The alleyway stank of seaweed and urine. I gagged and held my breath.

Behind us someone gave a shout. They'd found our footprints.

"Quick – follow me." I started to run, the mud pulling at the soles of my feet like greedy hands.

The alleyway opened up into a forecourt, littered with the scattered remains of forklift trucks, their lower halves encrusted with slimy green weed and barnacles.

We darted between the vehicles. Voices sounded in the alleyway behind us.

Then I saw the stream.

"There," I said, hope giving me a burst of speed. I started to run towards it – a stream of water flowing through the mud. It didn't occur to me that it was flowing uphill, tiny wavelets lapping at the mud, extending its width. All I could think was that it would hide our footprints.

I waded into it, trying not to splash. The water was ice cold and trickled over the tops of my boots, soaking my socks, but it led out of the forecourt and into another area of housing.

Gracie was close behind me, splashing more than she needed.

I started to run, but the water was getting deeper. The stream divided into two.

"Take the left," Gracie called. I didn't hesitate. I plunged forwards. Then the ground dropped away from underneath me and I gasped. I was standing in freezing water up to my waist.

Even as I stood, I could feel it creeping higher around me and when I looked around it had spread. The whole area of mudflats between the buildings was now a watercourse.

"The tide's running," said Gracie.

She started to wade towards the nearest building. It was old and stone-faced and I could see from the stain on the walls how high the water would reach.

These buildings would be cut off from one another. They would become islands and we would be trapped.

I waded after her. Then there were steps under my feet and I staggered upwards, out of the icy brine towards a door that hung broken from a single hinge.

I pushed it aside and slipped in.

Gracie followed me up the stairs, her shoes making a weird squelching noise. I was shivering, my teeth chattering and the more I tried to calm the shaking, the worse it got.

We stopped on the second floor. Another broken door led into a large room. Shattered windows down one side looked out over the city. The remains of desks and smashed computers littered the floor. This had been an office once, but a very long time ago. It had been pretty thoroughly picked over by now and it stank.

I moved over to the window and looked out. The city was just the tops of buildings sticking out of a rippling sea: all the roads, all the cars now covered. The sea was reclaiming it. Before long, the buildings would crumble and the city would be gone.

"I think that's where we're going," I said, pointing towards a tall set of spires. Gracie joined me, staring out across the flooded city. Water dripped from our jeans to form a puddle by our feet.

"So, that's the college where Lucy says she hid the thesis." Then she lowered her voice. "If it's still there." I don't think she wanted me to hear, but I did.

For a moment, we stood watching the water rise.

Then something rustled behind us.

"Who are you?" snarled an angry voice from the shadows.

11
Floodwater

I spun round, peering into the shadows.

"Who's there?"

For a moment there was silence. Then a pile of papers and rags shifted under one of the old desks. I squinted as a shape emerged, rising up to form a grimy, ragged man. His eyes darted from side to side like a trapped animal.

"This is my patch."

I pressed myself against the window sill, cold air on my back. "We're not going to stay. We'll be gone as soon as the tide drops."

"Are you alone?" Gracie asked, moving closer to me.

"What's it to you?" The man narrowed his eyes and watched us, flexing his fingers at his sides.

"You are, aren't you?" I said. He glanced over from the window to the door, but he didn't run.

"It's all right," I whispered. "We're not going to hurt you."

He took a step away from us. "They'll come looking for you." He checked his escape route again.

"Who will?" Gracie asked.

"Them – they don't welcome strangers."

"Scavvers?" I whispered.

The man hunched down slightly and shook his head.

"I'm a scavver, too. If you must call us that."

Gracie pressed closer and I could feel her shaking through the wool of my jumper.

The man wiped his nose on the back of his sleeve leaving a long shining streak.

"But you're different," I said.

"We're all trying to survive in our own way. There are no rules in the flooded areas." He looked up at me from hollow eyes, the fear in them gradually fading.

"Do they have boats?" I asked. He wrung his hands together and nodded.

I looked at Gracie, then took a deep breath and stepped towards the man. He shrank back before me. I thought he was about to crawl under his desk.

"Are you hungry?"

The man nodded again, a wild tangle of hair falling across his face.

"We have some spare food." I reached into my bag and pulled out a tin of beans. I held it up for him to see. His eyes glinted as I opened the can and handed it to him.

He took it and shrank back under the table. A moment later, I heard the tap of a spoon on tin and his ravenous slurping.

"Come on," said Gracie, shifting from foot to foot. "Let's get going."

"Just a minute," I said. The man had finished his beans and was looking out at me again.

"Do you have any more food?" he asked, wiping his mouth with the back of his hand.

"I have some biscuits." I fished into my bag.

The man smiled, deep creases lining his eyes. "Custard creams are my favourite."

"Danni."

There was something in her voice.

Gracie was staring out of the window, her body rigid and her eyes wide.

I looked out through the broken glass, and there it was: one of the old river punts approaching us over the water.

There were four men in it, two standing at either end pushing the boat along with their long poles and another two crouching in the bottom of the punt.

All four were staring straight at us.

"Oh my God!" gasped Gracie. "They can see us."

Another punt came into view from behind a nearby building, and then another.

"Quick, away from the window." The words came out of my mouth like a hiss.

We hurried back, but I heard a shout from below. The tramp emerged from his hiding place. He stood tall, his rags hanging from his gaunt frame.

"Is there another way out?" I asked.

He paused a moment, his eyes fixed on mine, and in that instant I could see the man he must have once been.

"This way," he said, and darted for the door.

He led us down the stairs. I could hear voices, the gentle slap of the wavelets against the stone steps and the rustle and swish of ropes being pulled through the water and secured.

"Here."

There was a cupboard or storage room. The door was hanging loose, but the deep shadow inside might be enough to hide us. I squeezed myself into the space and Gracie squirmed in beside me.

"Stay here. I'll draw them away." He started to push the door closed.

"Thank you," I whispered. But the door was closed and he had gone.

Below, voices echoed in the stairwell along with the sound of footsteps on stone.

I hardly dared breathe.

The footsteps sounded on the landing outside, and paused. I bit on my lip to stop my teeth from chattering.

Then came the sound of smashing glass upstairs.

"Next floor," said a voice, and the footsteps continued up the stairs. I let out a long, slow breath. A few moments later a floorboard creaked on the floor above. They were in the office.

"Now," I said.

We crept out of our hiding place. Gracie was so close that she almost stepped on my heels. My heart was beating hard, as though my chest was going to explode.

All I could hear was the scrape of footsteps above and the lapping water outside. A rope creaked as one of the punts pulled against its mooring.

A gruff voice sounded somewhere in the building and I flinched. Then came a wail of pleading followed by thuds and more angry voices.

"Run!" I started bounding down the steps two at a time.

Footsteps pounded above us and a voice called out, but I couldn't tell what was said. I leaped the last few steps.

Ahead of me was the door, still hanging, half broken. I crashed into it and yelped as my collarbone knocked against it. The door creaked and fell backwards with a splash. The water was now seeping over the threshold.

"The boats," I shouted.

Gracie pulled out her hunting knife and slashed at the ropes. One of the punts began to drift free. Then another. They started to float with the tide, slow to pull away at first, but the gap widened fast.

Gracie kept hold of the rope of the last of the punts. I jumped aboard, crouching low as it rocked back and forth. Gracie tumbled in a heap beside me. She struggled to her feet, picked up one of the poles and started to push the boat away.

I looked up. They were there on the steps, faces red and fists clenched in rage. One of them was wading into the water, reaching for the nearest boat.

I struggled to my feet and grabbed a second pole. The punt rocked beneath me and I spread my feet wide to balance. Then I jabbed at the boat he was reaching for, giving it a prod to help it on its way.

It hesitated a moment then spun out of reach as if caught in an eddy. His hand closed on empty air and he stumbled forwards into deeper water with a splash of salt spray.

He cursed me, his voice filled with hate, the sound of it making my skin crawl.

"Use your pole to push the boat," said Gracie. I looked across at the way she dug her pole into the water, then levered the boat forwards. I copied her and we picked up speed.

"They're swimming after the boats," I warned.

"We've got a head start though. Where now?"

I paused for a second while I fumbled with the damp pages of the map.

"This way."

We steered the boat up a narrow side street between tall terraced houses, then past one of the university colleges that rose out of the waters like some sort of mermaid fortress.

At one point, we heard voices and pulled in beside a high brick wall. We waited, but the sound came to nothing.

"Nearly there," I said. "In here."

We pulled up at the back of one of the old buildings. This one appeared to be permanently flooded and I could see by the damp tide line around its walls that the waters were beginning to recede.

There was a large opening which had once been a window. Gracie steered the boat inside, ducking low as we passed beneath the lintel.

We were in a large hall, the water lapping at the swollen wooden panels and the stairs beyond.

"Is this it?" Gracie asked.

I nodded. "I think so."

We tied the boat up at the foot of the stairs and crept up into the building.

"Do you have that piece of paper Lucy gave you?" Gracie whispered.

I pulled it from my pocket. It was soaking wet, but I prised it open. "Any guesses as to where this library is?"

"We'll need a scuba kit if it's in the basement."

"Sorry, you'll just have to hold your breath."

"Me? No chance." She took the sodden piece of paper from

my hand, turned it around a couple of times then handed it back.

"Let's try upstairs first," I said.

I wandered along the corridor. So this was where Robert and Lucy had studied, all those years ago. I half expected to see him walking towards me, laughing at my bedraggled state, teasing me like he always did. I tried to concentrate on the names on the doors, hoping I'd see something familiar.

And then I found it.

"In here."

I struggled to push open a heavy wooden door, swollen with damp. Inside was a large room with floor to ceiling bookcases, largely untouched, although the paper was peeling off the walls and the ceiling was green with mould.

It didn't look like the books were in a very good condition. Even if we found the thesis, I wasn't at all sure it would still be legible.

I stood in the middle of the room, shaking. Gracie shivered beside me.

"Right then, where do we start? What was the name of the book Lucy hid it behind?"

I studied Lucy's note. "Tacitus." I looked up at Gracie and shook my head. "I guess it could be anywhere?"

"No, Tacitus was a Roman historian." Gracie was already studying the bookshelves. "We need to find where the books on Roman history are."

I started to search the lines of volumes, running my finger along their spines.

Gracie moved over to the shelves on the opposite side of the room. "Greek history, Greek history – here – Roman history."

I joined her. "Good stuff. Pull them out. It should be behind."

I found the works by Tacitus and added them to the pile by our feet. Soon the shelf was half empty. There was nothing else there.

"Maybe there's another section on Rome?" Gracie suggested.

I shook my head. "No. It has to be here."

I reached my hand in and felt towards the back of the shelf. There was a gap before the wall. My heartbeat quickened.

"Maybe it fell down."

I dropped to my knees on the squelching carpet and started to drag out more books. These were large atlases, heavy with damp. I peered into the space behind. There was something there. I held my breath and pulled it out. It was a doctoral thesis, bound in a bottle green cover.

"Is that it?" asked Gracie.

I tried to open it. A piece of the cover tore off in my hand. The pages were all stuck together like pulp. I took a deep breath.

"It's ruined," I said.

"You don't think we could dry it out?"

"Maybe. We can try – perhaps enough to find some answers, anyway." I tucked it away under my jacket.

"Come on, let's get out of this city."

Get out of this city. It sounded so easy.

But MEXA were still out there – still out there and watching for us.

12
Mudflats

We clattered down the stairs. The boat was still there, bobbing gently on the tide.

I steadied myself to step aboard and froze. Something splashed into the water outside. I looked over at Gracie. Please, not those men – they'd have us trapped in here.

I held out one hand, signalling her to stand still and I listened with every nerve tingling.

Another splash, but this time accompanied by the flapping of wings as something outside took flight.

I lowered my hand. "Just gulls."

We crept onto the boat. Gracie took up a punting pole and I crouched low midway along, clutching the thesis to my chest. The water lapped against the bow and the scrape of the pole against the stone walls seemed louder than ever. I was convinced that the whole world could hear us.

We eased our way out through the open window, the sill

scraping the bottom of the boat. The sound jarred like chalk on a blackboard. If the tide had dropped any lower we would have been stuck.

And then we were back out in the thin sunshine and the breeze stirred the strands of loose hair across my face. The wind against my wet clothes chilled me and I started to shiver.

Gracie glanced over at the sound of my chattering teeth. She concentrated on pushing the punt as hard as she could.

It wasn't long before we beached it on the mudflats – mudflats that had once been a high street. I looked at the rows of buildings. One had been an off-licence, another a charity shop, now peeling paint and broken signs. I tried to imagine what it had looked like before, thronging with people, cars and bicycles. Perhaps Robert and Lucy had shopped here? But now the shop windows were jagged, broken panes of glass. The shops themselves formed dark caverns in which anything might be lurking.

I didn't want to think about what might be watching us. I just wanted to get as far away from this husk of a city as possible.

But we could go no further. The time had come to abandon our boat. I jumped down into the mud. It closed round my calves with a sucking squelch. Liquid seeped into my boots.

Gracie eased herself down into the grey slime and pulled a face. For a moment I wanted to laugh. But there could be people watching us. Laughter would have to wait.

"This way." I started to make my way through the mud. I lifted my legs high in exaggerated strides, all the while watching those empty dark buildings that lined the road, lobes of mud spilling into them through broken doors. Soon the sea and the tides would claim this city. All this history would be forgotten.

The mud thinned and soon there was solid ground beneath my feet. I studied the map again and led us on through the city, trying to skirt round where the scavvers had been. Except now – thinking back to the man who had helped us in that derelict building – they had lost some of their menace. After all, they were only people trying to survive in this changing world.

Narrow streets gave way to tree-lined avenues, and at last we were in the open fields. In the distance, I could see the blue shadow of a line of trees. That was the copse where the land rover waited. I quickened my pace.

It was still there, just as we had left it. My hands were shaking as Gracie started the engine.

She was smiling at me. "We did it."

We soon left the forest track and took to the open road. I wanted to put as much distance as possible between us and Cambridge. That mattered more than any bandits we might meet on the road. Bandits or worse. MEXA would be looking for us.

My teeth chattered. Gracie leaned over and turned up the heating. I rummaged through the glove compartment and held up a wad of notes.

"Looks like there're some shops up ahead. Let's stop and get some dry clothes."

"What? Here?" Gracie frowned at the row of shabby looking shops.

"Yes. Pull over. Maybe they sell hats."

We pulled up in front of a charity shop.

Gracie grimaced."But the clothes will be horrible!"

"They'll be cheap. And anyway, you can sometimes find really good stuff in these places."

"Oh, so you shop in places like this often, do you?" she said as she followed me into the shop. "That explains a lot."

"Oi," I said, pretending to take a swing at her. She giggled and ducked out of the way. It was good to be laughing like this, to feel normal again.

We wandered up and down between the racks of clothes. Everything was jumbled together in no particular order. Gracie lifted a floral dress off the rack and pulled a face.

"That really suits you," I said. "You should try it on."

"Maybe not." She put it back and went on rummaging.

I found some jeans and T-shirts that were my size. Gracie still didn't look terribly impressed.

Then I found a hat. It was made of orange canvas and had a wide floppy brim that drooped down over my eyes as I grinned at Gracie.

She gave me the thumbs up. "I like that better than the old one."

"I like hats. I've got stacks at home. Shall I find you one?" Mentioning home brought on that familiar pang: memories of everyone laughing, so vivid they hurt.

"I'll pass. I don't suit hats," said Gracie.

I found a fairly decent pair of trainers and checked them for size against my feet. Gracie dug out a pair of designer jeans and turned to me and smiled.

"Okay, I'll give you this one. You were right." She moved over to a shelf of toiletries.

The lady at the till eyed Gracie up and down as I handed

over Lucy's cash. She was mud-smeared and dishevelled. I probably looked just as bad.

"Would you like to get changed here?" she said, one eyebrow raised. "I won't ask what happened to you."

"Please, if it's no trouble."

"Through the back."

There was a large heavy curtain separating the front of the shop from the storage and sorting area behind. There was also a small kitchen and a toilet.

I put on the new clothes, swapping my phone into my dry pocket. The postcard and photo of my family were with it and I stared with dismay at the photograph, water-stained and ruined. I could barely make anyone out any more. Still, I didn't have the heart to throw it away.

I scrubbed my face and hands clean, although some of the grime around my fingernails was pretty ingrained. There wasn't much that I could do about my hair. I scraped it back off my face and tied it up but I could still smell seaweed.

Gracie washed her face, tied her hair back into a knot and inspected herself in the mirror. With clean dry clothes on she looked perfectly normal.

I still looked a state.

Then she produced some mascara. I'm sure my mouth fell open. She spotted me looking and smiled.

"Well, you never know," she said as she unscrewed the lid. "There might be some fit blokes when we get to the pub." And then she laughed. "Look at me! I stink of seaweed. I don't think a bit of mascara is going to make much difference."

I smiled. "Not unless they like fish."

"You do look a mess still," Gracie said and giggled. "Here, let me try."

She pulled out a handful of paper towels and soaked them in the sink. Then she set about cleaning me up, like a small child. I wriggled and giggled.

"There, that's better," said Gracie, stepping back to admire her handiwork. Then she sprayed me with perfume.

"That's rank," I spluttered.

"Better than 'eau de seaweed'."

"We should go to that pub," I said, adjusting the angle of my new hat. "We could really use that fake ID, and some credit."

I looked down at the change in my hand. There wasn't much of Lucy's money left.

13
The Thesis

After about an hour we pulled up at the pub.

"We'll get something to eat here," Gracie said as I followed her inside. I was still certain that I smelled of seaweed.

It was one of those pubs with old oak beams hung with horse brasses and a fire blazing in an open hearth. The seats nearest to the fire were free and I hurried over to claim them.

Gracie pulled the thesis from under her jacket and laid it out on the table in front of us.

"Hungry?" she said. "I'll go and see what's on the menu."

I pulled out the sodden photograph and postcard and laid them by the thesis to dry out. Then I settled back in my seat and took out my phone.

Isaac – he'd be wondering why I hadn't called. I pressed the 'on' switch but nothing happened. A large drop of salty water landed on the floor between my feet. I shook it and tried again, but it was no good. My phone was dead.

Gracie came back with the drinks and a broad smile. "I hope you don't mind, but I ordered for you. There wasn't a lot of choice."

She threw herself down into the chair opposite. "I asked at the bar. The guy didn't know about any package, but he's going to check."

Maybe Lucy had forgotten her promise, or maybe it hadn't arrived yet. Fake ID would have been useful. I guessed we'd just have to manage without. Lack of money was going to be more of a problem.

Gracie nodded towards the book.

"Bit of a state, isn't it?"

I gave it a prod. "Maybe it'll be fine once it's dried out a bit." But looking at it lying there, a white crust of salt starting to appear on the bottle green cover, I didn't hold out much hope.

Gracie pulled back the cover, but the binding fell apart in her hands.

"That's not good. The library was just too damp. It's tragic really, all those beautiful books."

I pulled a knife out of my cutlery pack and eased it between the sodden pages. I tried to gently prise the pages apart, pausing every now and then to let the warmth dry them a bit more.

"This is pretty much mush," I said after a few minutes as the waitress brought our food over, two steaming platefuls of pie and mash. "I'm not sure we're going to salvage much."

We ate in silence. I shifted the table closer to the fire and we sat and watched as the pages of the book started to curl in the warmth. My stomach full, I started to feel sleepy, what with the glow of the fire and the gentle throb of the jukebox.

My head nodded and jerked me awake. I wasn't sure how long I'd been asleep.

Gracie was over by the door. I could just see the back of her head as she fumbled with something on the wall in front of her.

I straightened up in my seat and tried to get a better look. She was fiddling around with an old pay phone. The handset was up by her ear.

She looked round and when she saw me watching she put it down, clunking it into its cradle and came back over to our table.

"What were you doing, Gracie?"

"Just seeing if that old thing works."

"And does it?" If it did, I could call Isaac.

But Gracie shook her head. "'Fraid not." She sat back down and pointed at the pages in front of her.

"Looks like the book's dried off a bit," she said.

I spread the remnants of the pages out across the table, moving them around with the tip of my forefinger.

"Most of it's completely ruined."

Gracie tipped one of the fragments towards the firelight, sighed and put it back down.

But some of the pages were still legible.

"Look at this," I said.

"What is it?"

"No idea." It was a picture – a sketch. I turned the page round to an angle, trying to make it out. "Looks like some weird sort of aircraft."

"It says it's a 'star chariot'." Gracie pointed to the text underneath.

I turned to the next semi-legible page. "This seems to be talking about some sort of disaster," I said. "Listen to this... '...*it spread like a plague until all the people were consumed by its madness, and the cities were swallowed by the drifting snows in the darkness of the age that followed...*'"

"What's that all about?" asked Gracie.

"No idea," I said, leafing through the fragile pages. "There's more stuff about this great cataclysm. Maybe this is what happened to those bodies we found."

"Could be."

"And this section seems to be speculating about where the ruins might be."

"The ruins that we found?" Gracie was smiling.

"Ah, this looks like the acknowledgments page," I said. I tipped my head to one side and peered at the paper. A few fragments of sentence were still legible. "'...*thank my tutor Professor Douglas...*' Can we ask him?" I suggested.

Gracie looked doubtful. "If we can find him."

"'...*and for his help deciphering the texts, my sincere gratitude to the Abbot of Saint Publius...*' Saint who?" I asked.

She turned over another page. "It's in Malta. '*and my thanks to the Maltese Government for granting me access to these ancient writings.*'."

She looked at me wide-eyed.

"We've got to go to Malta. I've always wanted to go there."

Gracie's eyes were shining, the corners of her mouth turned up in a smile.

But I wasn't smiling. Far from it. My head was spinning

and something stung at the back of my throat.

Oak beams and horse brasses blurred into one with the bar and the fireplace. I couldn't go to Malta.

How could I possibly go to the place where my parents had died?

This couldn't be a coincidence – could it? I was making all sorts of scary connections. The more I thought about it, the more my head started to spin.

Gracie was looking at me. I tried to stand up, but my legs gave way under me. The carpet was rough and red and covered with a swirling pattern. And it was rushing to meet me – coarse against my cheek. I closed my eyes. It smelled of damp dog and cinders.

"Danni."

There was a hand on my shoulder. The hand shook me and I flinched, screwing my eyes tight. The ache in my chest was back. I missed them so much, it hurt. I wished I could vanish and leave the pain behind.

"Danni, try to sit up."

She tugged on my arm, heaving me upright, and pressed a glass of water against my lips. It slid down my throat like liquid frost. My head stopped spinning and I opened my eyes.

"Are you okay?" asked Gracie.

"I'll be fine," I said, trying to sound convincing.

"Do you want to stay here a bit longer?"

I shook my head. "No, let's go."

She helped me to my feet. Some of the people sitting around had been staring at me, but quickly turned away.

As we passed the bar, someone spoke.

"You Danni Rushton?"

I froze. Had MEXA caught up with us already?

But it was only the barman holding a package out towards me. He smiled, a gap-toothed grin. Lucy hadn't let us down.

"Thanks," I murmured and followed Gracie out to the land rover.

"We'll find somewhere to camp nearby," she said as she struggled with the gears. "And tomorrow we'll head for the airport."

She sounded so eager, but I didn't have the strength left to argue.

I took a deep breath and ran my fingers over Lucy's package. This time MEXA wouldn't trace us. I reached up and touched the object round my neck, sharp beneath my jumper. So much trouble over something so small.

I tried not to think about where we were going.

14
Doubts

I sat in a daze as Gracie drove down twisting tracks. All I could think of was my parents and Kris. I felt I was choking, I missed them so much.

Dusk was already closing in when we finally stopped. We were in the corner of a field, woodland on one side, a stream on the other. Gracie climbed down from the land rover and stretched, arms above her head, reaching towards a sky that seethed dark and threatened rain.

I didn't move. My head was spinning. Everything was happening so fast. I had been so certain, but now I wasn't feeling sure of myself.

Gracie looked round at me, and I could see the concern in her eyes. She came over to my side and opened the door.

"Are you all right?"

"I don't know." I shivered at the blast of chill air.

"What's wrong?"

I shook my head and ran my hands over the package Lucy had left for us. "What are we doing, Gracie?" I whispered.

"What do you mean?"

I picked at the tape with my fingernail. "I was so sure that we'd find the answers in Cambridge."

"We found the thesis."

"But it hasn't led us to Robert. He could be anywhere and we still don't know why MEXA took him." A couple of raindrops landed on the windscreen. Just like tears. I blinked, trying to keep my own eyes from brimming over.

"Everything in the thesis points towards Malta," said Gracie, her voice strangely eager. "That's where we should go next."

"I can't go to Malta," I said, looking up and meeting her eye. "It's where my parents died."

I felt myself choking up as I said those words. Gracie's eyes opened wide. I took a deep breath.

"Gracie, what are we even going to do if we go there?"

"Look for your uncle?" she suggested.

"But what if he isn't in Malta? I should have gone straight to the police! What if he's already dead?" My voice shook. I wasn't yet ready to face that possibility.

Gracie took hold of my hand. "Don't think that way. We'll find him."

A large tear trickled down my cheek. More rain hit the windscreen.

"But how are we going to get there? Who's going to pay for our flights?"

Gracie rubbed her hand up and down my arm.

"Open the package. Let's see what Lucy has left us."

I picked at the packing tape. Gracie took it off me and slit it open with her hunting knife. Inside were two ID cards and a wad of cash. She thumbed through the money and handed it to me. Then she inspected the cards.

"Awful photographs," she said with a smile, handing me mine. "Looks like they're stills taken by the CCTV cameras above the guard's office in the MI5 building."

"I'm 'Amanda Jones'," I said with a half smile. Gracie was right. It really was an appalling picture.

Gracie pulled a face. "'Fionnula Snodgrass'. Oh, for goodness' sake. Couldn't she come up with anything better! 'Amanda Jones' is okay!"

I giggled. Lucy always did have a weird sense of humour.

"She's given us a decent amount of credit though," said Gracie.

I checked the LED readout on the card. "I guess it's enough to keep us going for a couple of weeks while she sorts stuff out."

"Or enough to pay for our flights to Malta," said Gracie.

"And then what?" I asked. "Gracie, I don't have a plan or anything. What are we going to do when we get to Malta? We'll be using all this money on the flights alone." I waved my new ID card with one hand and pointed at the cash on the seat beside me with the other. "We won't even have money for a hotel."

Gracie smiled, her eyes narrow and glinting. "Don't worry about that. One of my cousins runs a small hotel in Malta. He'll let us stay, and he won't ask any questions. I can probably even persuade him to stand us some cash."

"But won't that be dangerous? What if MEXA trace us?"

"Trust me on this," said Gracie. "They won't." There was

an odd insistence in her voice. Of course I trusted her. She'd stuck by me when I had no one else. She was older than me. She was bound to know what she was doing.

I tucked the ID card away in my pocket, put the cash in the glove compartment and climbed down to join her on the soft grass. It was now almost dark and an owl let out its soft call from among the trees. The downpour that threatened had never materialised, but the ground was spongy and damp.

"Maybe we should do what Lucy told us to do and find somewhere to hide. Or maybe we should try to find the Professor who wrote the thesis?" I said.

"Did you see the date on that thing?" Gracie tipped her head to one side as the owl called again. "He's probably dead by now. No. I think our best bet is to find this monastery on Malta and speak to this abbot."

The thought of my parents crowded in on me, choking me. Was this really a coincidence? I didn't answer.

"Anyway," said Gracie. "Remember I told you how I wanted to go backpacking but my Dad wouldn't let me?"

"Did you?"

"Yes. Well, now is my chance. I really want to see Malta. I want to go somewhere on my own where I want to go, not where my Dad drags me because that's where his work takes him. And I want to help you find your uncle."

I smiled at her, although I knew that my smile was lost in the dark.

"Thank you, Gracie."

Gracie gave my shoulder a reassuring squeeze.

"So, grab a torch and help me find some firewood that isn't soaked," she said.

15

Malta

Our flight arrived in Malta the next evening. We found the hotel in one of the old tourist areas, now half empty. I picked up an old tourist guide in the foyer and sat flicking through it as Gracie chatted to her cousin on reception. He kept glancing over in my direction, which was oddly unnerving. After a few minutes, Gracie turned and gave me the thumbs up before vanishing into a back room with him.

I looked round at the peeling paint and cracked plaster. As far as I could tell, there weren't many other guests here. I began to wonder if this place was even open. But then Gracie returned clutching a room key and grinning broadly. I guessed she'd succeeded in tapping her cousin for cash.

When morning came, I stood on the hotel balcony watching the dawn light spread across the sky. It was warm already, that lovely fresh warmth that hinted at the scorcher to come.

I held the postcard my parents had sent me in my hand and tried not to cry. The water in Cambridge had damaged it, blunting the corners and staining the picture, but I could still make out the writing on the back. The last words my mother had ever written to me. Everything was connected. I knew that now. Their death, Kris's death, Robert and MEXA. It was all swirling round and round in my head. Had they really been on a diving holiday? Or had Robert sent them here?

I reached up and tugged on the cord around my neck. Was everyone dying because of this stone? Was I going to be next? And what *was* this stone Kris had given me? There was something more to all this and I had to know the truth, about Kris, about my parents – about everything.

Gracie's voice was bleary with sleep. "Did you sleep okay?" she asked, joining me on the balcony.

I hadn't slept a wink. I kept thinking about my parents, those caves and that island. Trying not to imagine what it must have been like for them as their air ran out. Gasping in the dark as their lights failed.

"Isn't this great?" Gracie leaned over and looked down into the streets below. "I've always wanted to come on holiday to Malta."

"Holiday?"

She nudged me with her elbow. "Oh, don't look so serious. So it's not exactly a holiday, but we might as well make the most of it while we're here."

"Okay, okay. But let's find what we came for first."

"Alright, where do we start?" Gracie said with a yawn.

I took a deep breath. "We need to visit St Publius's. It's a monastery." I gestured towards the tourist guide on my bed.

"On the island of Comino."

"Comino?" Gracie flicked through the pages.

I swallowed. I wasn't going to tell her. Why did the monastery have to be there? There was a knot in my throat but I was determined not to cry.

"We can charter a boat," said Gracie. "We'll go down to the harbour straight after breakfast."

I shook my head. "It's not so easy. We can go to Comino right enough. Lots of people do. To visit the ruins. St Publius's is another matter."

"Why?" I knew she could tell that something was wrong. She didn't press me, though. I'll give her credit for that.

"St Publius's is sacred ground and only the monks can go in there. Ordinary people aren't allowed."

"Well, there must be a way," said Gracie. "Come on. Let's get down to breakfast."

I smiled. "You're right. We'll charter a boat and find out when we get there."

After a breakfast of yoghurt and oranges we walked down towards the harbour, through narrow streets, washing strung between the windows overhead. Voices of women and children sounded from open doorways.

I looked at the buildings as we passed. Maybe somewhere here was a shop where I could buy a new phone. Isaac wanted me to call and I never had. But all we passed were dwellings. It would have to wait until we got back.

The harbour had probably once been a town square. The houses around were all half flooded and makeshift jetties had been built around the edge, jutting out from the sides of semi-submerged buildings. Of course, the original harbour had long since become unusable as the rising seas had smothered lower-lying districts.

But it wasn't as bad as some of the places I'd seen. Most of this town was on higher land, above the levels where the sea could reach. Only the lowest houses lay abandoned to the waves.

There were plenty of fishing boats to choose from. I stared around at them and an old man with white whiskers tipped his hat to me and smiled. I touched the rim of my own hat in reply.

Was I imagining it or was there a look of recognition in his eyes?

"Danni? It is Danni, isn't it?" he said in a strong Maltese accent.

I gave a quick glance over at Gracie. She hadn't noticed. She was talking to another fisherman and counting out money from the wad of notes her cousin had lent her. I turned back to him.

"How do you know who I am?"

"You look just like her."

I opened my eyes wide. "Who?"

"Why, your mother, of course."

For a moment I felt dizzy. "You knew my parents? You were here when…"

Gracie was climbing aboard a motor boat. She waved to me. "Come on."

"You should have a guide…" the fisherman said.

I glanced across at Gracie. Maybe he was right. But it was such a lovely fine day, and in any case, these days most people could handle a boat.

"…if you're thinking of going to Comino."

I froze. How did he…? I took a step away from him.

"Thanks," I said. "But it looks like my friend's already paid. And we're just going round the coast a bit anyway. We'll be fine."

"Well, any time you need a boat," said the fisherman.

"Okay. I'll remember that." I waved back at Gracie and started to run along the jetty towards her.

When I reached her, I looked back at the old man. He was still watching me. When he saw me look, he lifted his hand and mouthed something to me.

It looked like he was saying "Be careful, Danni," but I couldn't be sure.

16
Comino

It was lovely out on the water, with clear skies and a warm sun beating down on us as the heat of the day increased. I let my arm dangle over the side of the boat and felt the cool water slip between my fingers. The outboard engine throbbed and ahead I could see the island, rising pale and clear out of the haze that was forming over the surface of the sea.

I stared at those cream-coloured cliffs. There were caves there. Caves I hoped I would never have to see.

And I couldn't stop thinking about that fisherman back on Malta. Half of me wished I had stayed behind to talk. He knew my parents – knew a side of them I never had – had seen them after they had already gone from my life.

But Robert was still alive. Maybe. I couldn't help the dead, but perhaps I could help him. And if there was someone on this island who could tell me what this was all about then I had to know. Robert would want me to find out the truth, wouldn't he? What was it we had found in that cave? And why did MEXA want it so badly?

I squinted at the boats coming and going over the flat, calm water and fingered the postcard in my pocket. I knew by heart the cheery message my mother had written on the back:

"We're going to visit this old church tomorrow – Dad wants to look at some dusty old scrolls. Wish you could have come with us. All my love, Mum."

I was here now, but they were dead. Were these scrolls the answer? Was this what they came here for?

Gracie eased back on the throttle. The island was getting nearer.

She steered us into a rocky inlet, killed the engine and jumped onto the ledge we had pulled up alongside. It was a perfect landing place. Hidden from view. Only someone standing on the cliff right above us would know we were here.

"Good spot, Gracie." I said as I secured the boat, double checking my knots. I touched Kris's rock, which made a fairly obvious bulge under my T-shirt, and smoothed it down.

Maybe here we would find some answers.

We started to scramble up the rocky path. It was already hot and I was starting to sweat as I reached the cliff top. The rock up here had been cut into a patchwork of saltpans, some filled with water and others with dried white salt. The sun beat down on the top of my head and glared back at me off the limestone. I lowered the brim of my hat to help shield my eyes.

The cave where it had happened must be near here. Maybe

it was right underneath us? I tried to put the thought out of my mind, but it kept creeping back.

Think of something else. Think about getting the monks to talk to us.

The monastery was just ahead.

It wasn't as large as I had expected: a few stone buildings, one clearly a church, surrounded by a limestone wall. It had been built using the same stone that made up the island, causing it to blend into the landscape.

I pulled out the postcard and shivered. My parents had sent me a picture of the island where they were going to die. And now I was following them. But following them to what?

We started to pick our way across the saltpans. Soon they gave way to scrubby ground and as we drew nearer we passed patches of tomatoes and melons flourishing in the sunshine.

When we reached the walls of St Publius's I stopped, staring up at the pale stone facade. It was too high to climb.

"There must be a way in."

Gracie nodded. "Probably round the other side."

We started to track along the wall. At last we came to a large wooden door where a dusty road led away down the hill towards a group of buildings which, according to the guidebook, were a hotel and desalination plant. The place seemed deserted, but there was a bell pull hanging alongside.

I gave it a tug and the sound of a bell echoed behind the walls.

"Nobody home?" said Gracie after a couple of minutes.

"Probably at prayers." I reached out to ring again, but at that moment a hatch in the door slid open and a face peered out at us and started talking rapidly in Maltese.

"Do you speak English?" Gracie asked.

"Yes, I do. What are you doing here? What do you want?" His tone was gruff and unwelcoming.

"We need to speak to the abbot," I said, trying to keep my voice steady. "Please."

"You can't."

"But it's really important."

"Go away." The hatch slammed shut.

"I'll ring it again," said Gracie. She reached out, but I stayed her hand.

"Let's look around a bit more."

We followed the wall until we had done a full circuit of St Publius's. There were no other entrances.

But this time, as we reached the vegetable gardens, there were monks. They were dressed in brown robes and they were tending their plots. They didn't look up, but I'm pretty certain that they knew we were there. I walked up to one of them and he acted as if he couldn't see me.

"Hello," I said after a couple of minutes. He didn't respond. I felt a bit foolish, as if I was talking to empty space. I took a deep breath.

"We would very much like to talk to the abbot."

No answer.

"It's my uncle, you see. He's been captured and we think the abbot may be able to help us."

He turned away from me and continued hoeing.

"Your monastery is the only lead we have."

Silence, apart from the scrape scrape scrape of his hoe in the dusty earth.

Maybe I should try a different tack.

"Did some people come to see you? A man and a woman,

to see some scrolls?" This time, yes, a flick of his eyes and a stiffening in his shoulders.

All of a sudden, I felt cold. I was right. There was something more to my parents' death.

By now Gracie was beside me.

"Let me try," she whispered.

"No…" But she had already walked past me to put her hand on the monk's shoulder.

The monk spun round and his hoe clattered to the ground. He glared at her.

"Let go of me," he said.

She held up her hands and stepped back. "OK. But we just want to see the abbot."

"You can't," he spat.

He picked up his hoe, holding it like a weapon, and pointed it towards her.

"Leave this place."

Gracie backed into me and I stumbled and fell, sprawling on the dusty ground, the smell of crushed tomato plants all around me.

Gracie gave a little squeal. She put her hands over her mouth as I sat up, rubbing the back of my head where it had bumped on the ground.

Gracie and the monk were both staring at me. No, not at me, at my neck – at something around my neck.

I looked down.

Kris's rock had flopped out from my T-shirt as I fell and now it was lying on my chest in full view.

I grabbed it and tucked it out of sight.

The monk squatted on the dry ground beside me. He picked up my hat, dusted it down and handed it to me.

"You have the key." His voice was soft.

"Key?" I touched the object, now safe beneath cotton. It didn't look much like a key to me.

The monk straightened up and offered me his hand. He pulled me to my feet.

"I think you'd both better come with me."

17
The Abbot

The monk led us across a deserted courtyard and into a building that smelt of stale incense and dusty stone. I ran my fingers over the cold walls as we walked.

The abbot was at prayer, so the monk signalled to us that we should wait by the open door. He hurried into a small chapel, filled with flickering candlelight, bowed low and crossed himself. A hooded figure knelt before a small altar and I heard their voices, hushed whispers muttering in Maltese.

Then the abbot rose and they both came out to join us.

"Is this true?" asked the abbot, fixing me with a hard stare. His eyes were dark shadows beneath his hood.

"Show him," said the monk. His eyes darted back and forth from me to the abbot.

I pulled the rock out from my T-shirt and held it up for him to see. I held it firm, wary, ready to snatch it back. But he made no move to touch it. He nodded slowly and pushed back his hood to reveal a mop of white hair. The creases at the corners of his eyes deepened as he squinted at the rock.

Then he shook his head as if he couldn't believe what he was seeing.

"Follow me," he said.

He led us along a narrow corridor and dust stirred beneath our feet. The corridors were narrow and we had to stoop under shrouds of cobwebs. Nobody had come this way in a very long time.

At last the abbot pushed open a door to a musty room, lined with shelves of old books. He opened the shutters and sunlight streamed in.

There was no dust in this room.

The abbot turned towards us.

"You must be Danni Rushton," he said.

I stared at him, open-mouthed. How had he known that?

He smiled at the look on my face.

"We may live in a remote place, but we do keep abreast of world affairs," he said. "I was so sorry to hear about your aunt."

"How did you?"

"The assassination of one of the crew of the first Mars Mission is bound to make the headlines."

I flinched. I hadn't expected him to use the word 'assassination'. So he suspected something, too.

"And your friend?"

"This is Gracie."

Gracie gave him a warm smile.

I touched my hand to my chest.

"The monk called it a 'key'," I said. It was as much a

question as a statement.

"Where did you find it?" His voice was firm, commanding.

"I didn't." I glanced round at Gracie. Then turned back to the abbot. "My aunt, Kris. She gave it to me before she died."

"And did she say anything about it?"

I shook my head.

The abbot pressed the palms of his hands together, as if in prayer." I never thought I would see it with my own eyes. I am glad you brought it here. Here, it will be safe."

"Safe?" I tightened my fingers around it. "What do you mean?"

"I mean that it must stay here, where no one can touch it. It should, of course, have been left where it was."

"Where Kris found it?"

"Yes," said the abbot. "On Mars."

"Mars?" I stared at him. "I thought it came from Greenland?" But as I spoke it all started to make horrible sense. Kris dying in Robert's arms, the blood soaking into her jumper. She had only just returned from Mars. I looked across at Gracie. She didn't look surprised.

"Well, it did come from Greenland originally," said the abbot.

"But then how did it get to Mars? Did Kris take it there?"

"No. She found it there."

"On Mars? That's crazy. And anyway, the chances of the Mars Mission just happening to land..."

"Not if that is what MEXA were looking for in the first place." His eyes were fixed on me.

I laughed. "They wouldn't mount a trip to Mars just to look for a piece of rock. The Mars Mission was about much more than that."

"Was it?" said the abbot, raising one eyebrow. I clasped the stone so tight it started to cut into my fingers. Whatever it was, he wasn't getting his hands on it.

"Let me show you," said the abbot. He took a large leather-bound box from one of the shelves and laid it out on the desk. He pulled on a pair of white silk gloves, carefully adjusting each finger in turn. Then he opened the box. I leaned over. Inside was a scroll.

"This scroll is very ancient," he said. "It has been transcribed many times, and all copies are kept locked away in this very monastery. But I thought you would like to see the oldest copy we hold."

"The original?" asked Gracie.

The abbot flashed her a smile.

"By no means," he said. "This is the oldest copy that exists today, but it has been transcribed many times before and into many different languages. Much of the content is lost. But enough remains. This text is in Phoenician."

"Who wrote it?" I asked.

"The last remnants of an ancient civilisation ended up here. These are their records." He stepped back from the scroll for us to see. We moved forwards, Gracie pressing close to me as she strained for a better look. There, on the page before me, was a picture of the same object I wore around my neck. There was writing beneath it in a script I could not read.

"What does it say?" I asked, my heart pounding.

"It says this is a picture of the key."

"Key to what?" I asked, reaching up to touch the stone, pressing it into my skin.

"What else does it say?" said Gracie, leaning over in front

of me.

"It says how the Proto People sent the sacred key on one of their chariots to the stars so that it would be hidden from the world."

"Proto People?" I said. My heart was thumping. "That's what Robert called the bodies we found at the dig in Greenland."

"So who were these people?" asked Gracie. "The bodies didn't look human."

"That's right," said the abbot. "They weren't."

The abbot unrolled the scroll to a different section. Now we could see more pictures and more writing.

"It is our greatest vanity to assume that we are the only species to have developed an advanced technological civilisation on this planet," he said. "Whilst our ancestors were still languishing on some African plain, a race of hominids that came before us developed an advanced society. We call them the Proto People."

"They built the city we found in Greenland." I marvelled, the pieces of information clicking together. I was speaking to myself as much as anyone, but the Abbot gave me a sharp look.

"So their city has been uncovered?" He nodded slowly. "Their main centre of civilisation was indeed the land we now call Greenland, where they lived the last time the ice caps had retreated far enough. Tell me, what else did you find?"

I swallowed. "Broken pieces of something, rocks with strange writing on them."

"And these rocks?"

"MEXA took them."

"MEXA?" The abbot's eyes narrowed. "Then it is essential that the key remains here. It should have been left on Mars."

Mars again. As if!

"How could such an ancient people possibly send the key to Mars?"

The abbot seemed amused by my exasperation. "Danni, it is written that they rode their chariots between the stars. This was no race of Stone Age or even Iron Age technology. No. They were far more advanced than that. They developed a technology far beyond anything that our species has so far managed to achieve. As I said before, it is our greatest vanity to assume that we are the pinnacle of evolution."

"What sort of technology?" I asked. I stared at the writing in front of me. I wanted to reach out and touch it, but the abbot was wearing silk gloves, and I knew that I mustn't.

"Space flight for a start," said the abbot, giving me a patient smile. "But much more. Technology that we cannot even begin to comprehend."

"And is that what you think MEXA are after? Their technology?"

"I believe so."

"But what for?"

The abbot shook his head. "Only MEXA know the answer to that."

"But if the Proto People were in Greenland, then how come you have the scripts here?" I asked. So many questions were buzzing round in my head.

The abbot smiled. "At the end, during the cataclysm, the survivors scattered across the globe. A few took refuge on these islands. Here, they inscribed their history onto the walls of caves. Those were the scripts discovered and translated by the earliest people on these islands. Many of the original cave writings have now been lost, but our order grew up to protect the ancient knowledge held within these texts."

"What happened to them?" I asked. "What was this cataclysm?"

"It's unclear." He shrugged. "They paid the price of their arrogance and brought down a great disaster upon themselves. Their writings speak of a creeping madness that consumed their kind. Sometimes they call it the Slow Dying. At other times they speak of a catastrophic event back home in their city."

"So some of them survived?"

"Not for long." He moved the scroll on to another section, more diagrams, illustrations of fragments of rock, marked with strange lines. I couldn't help wondering if this was some kind of instruction manual. "This text, however, only speaks of their greatest invention, of which this key was part. An invention that was going to transform their civilisation forever. "

"And the key?"

He rolled the scroll further open and, there, in the next section, were more pictures of the same fragments, but this time showing how they fitted together like a puzzle. And at the centre of them all was the key. Kris's key. And the fragments – they looked just like the pieces Gracie and I had found in that underground cavern.

"The fragments of rock and the key are sacred artefacts," he said. "The key should never have been brought back. They sent it away to a distant world to keep this one safe. But now you have brought it to us, it must stay."

"Does it say how the machine works?" asked Gracie.

"Machine?" I looked up at her. There was a strange intensity in her eyes. The abbot was frowning at her.

"Your questions tell me a lot about you," he said, his voice sounding tighter, strained. He rolled up the scroll. "They tell me that perhaps you haven't been entirely honest with me."

"Of course we have," said Gracie. The abbot turned to me.

"Kris gave me the key before she died," I said, my voice shaking. "She told me to tell no one."

I watched the abbot rub his chin and nod.

"What is this machine? What does it...?" I started to ask. But the abbot was no longer looking at me. He was staring at Gracie and his eyes were wide.

Gracie had drawn a gun and was pointing it straight at him.

18
Girl with a Gun

I turned to Gracie. The gun trembled ever so slightly in her grasp.

"Gracie?" I gasped. "What are you doing?"

"You are making a terrible mistake," said the abbot, holding his hands out towards her. "Please. Give that to me."

Gracie's face twisted into an awkward smile. "Put the scroll back into the box." Her voice was barely more than a whisper.

"Gracie, where did you get that gun?" My voice was shaking. What was Gracie playing at?

She didn't answer but used both hands to hold her aim steady.

"You cannot read it," said the abbot. "It will be of no use to you."

"I don't need to read it. It's the diagrams I want. They show how it all fits together. And the key. Now we have everything we need."

"But you don't understand," said the abbot, a note of desperation creeping into his voice. "Mankind isn't ready for this..."

He never finished. A loud crack sounded and the abbot's eyes opened wide. Behind his shoulder a bullet hole punctured the plaster. A small cloud of dust drifted in the sunlight.

"Give me the scroll," said Gracie, the gun wobbling in her clasp.

The abbot hesitated. Then he put his hands behind his back and lifted his head to look her in the eye.

"No."

"Now." The pitch of her voice had risen slightly. "I won't aim to miss next time."

"How could you, Gracie?" I started. But then the gun was pointing at me.

"Danni, pick up the scroll." Her voice was flat.

"You'd better do as she says," said the abbot. "I think she means it."

I picked up the box and scroll, tears burning my eyes.

Gracie's gun was pointing at my chest. She held out her hand.

"Give me the key."

I shook my head.

Her eyes narrowed slightly. "You don't have a choice."

I was shaking so badly I don't think I could have moved even if I'd wanted to.

"Why are you doing this, Gracie? I thought you were my friend."

A look of uncertainty flickered across her eyes. Her hands

started to shake and she adjusted her grip, trying to keep the gun steady.

"Gracie. Why?" It felt as if I was in a daze. This couldn't be happening.

Her bottom lip trembled.

"I- I- My father..." Gracie's voice faltered. She kept glancing over at the abbot, but he didn't move.

"Please, Gracie," I mouthed. "I don't want to die."

"I'm sorry, Danni," she said at last. "You have to come with me. They want to talk to you."

I had no doubt in my mind who "they" were. "They" had to be MEXA.

"You used me," I said, my voice quivering with rage and fear. "You used me to get to the scrolls. Kris was right to tell me not to trust anyone. And I should never have trusted you. I hate you!"

I spat the last words at her. Gracie took a step back. For a moment, she looked afraid.

"I have to do this," she mumbled.

Then she narrowed her eyes.

"If you come after us, I'll kill her," she said, turning back to the abbot. Her voice was strained, almost as if she didn't really mean it.

He blinked and shook his head.

She moved round behind me and the barrel of her gun jabbed into the small of my back.

"Nice and slowly now." She opened the door and peered out into the corridor. "It's clear."

Gracie pushed me ahead of her. The silence pressed in on me from all sides. The place was deserted.

We reached the courtyard. Ahead of us, across its dusty

emptiness, was the gate. A gate that led back out to the barren expanse of rock that formed this island. To the boat and whatever Gracie had planned for me.

But the courtyard wasn't empty. There was a monk there, right in the middle, harnessing a donkey to a cart.

He hadn't seen us. We watched from the shadows. The gun was hard against my spine.

"What now?" I whispered.

"We walk," said Gracie. "As if everything is normal." She jabbed the gun into my back and I flinched. Then she took the scroll box from me and tucked it under her arm. "And don't you go trying anything. Understand?"

We started out across the courtyard. Gracie put her gun out of sight, but I knew where it was aimed. My legs felt weak. I don't think I would have had the strength to run, even if I got the chance. Half of me still couldn't believe what was happening.

I stared hard at the monk, willing him to look in my direction, willing him to read the fear in my eyes. But he never once looked round. It was as if we didn't exist.

Gracie slid the bolts back on the gate and pushed me out of the monastery, out of the last sanctuary left. Any hope that we might pass some monks at work in the gardens soon faded. I stumbled on across the saltpans, the white crystals glaring at me.

We paused at the top of the cliff. Gracie held the gun in front of her.

"Go on," she said. "You go down first."

I stood my ground. She wouldn't really shoot me – would she? She took another step towards me.

"I will if I have to." The gun wobbled in her hand.

I turned and started to scramble down the cliff. The rocks scraped the skin off my palms and they stung with the salt of my sweat.

Behind me I heard Gracie clambering down, too. And then I heard her slip.

I looked back up the cliff.

Gracie was sitting down and a flurry of loose stone slid past me, skittering down to the rocks below. She was holding on with both hands to stop sliding any further – and she had dropped her gun. It was lying a short distance away. She had dropped the box as well and it had slid a little way from the path. Her eyes were wide, staring at me.

I didn't stop to think. I started climbing upwards, as fast as I could. She didn't move. She just clung there, watching me.

"Cow," I hissed as I pushed past her, giving the gun a hefty kick as I climbed.

I heard it bouncing off the rocks below as it fell. Even so, I half expected to feel the bite of a bullet at any moment. I reached the top of the cliff and started to run. Behind me was silence.

I splashed through the saltpans. There was no cover here. I searched as I ran, for something, anything.

Then ahead of me was a gully, a fissure in the limestone, and I dropped down into it.

There was sand along its base, as if a stream had once run here, and small scrubby plants clung to its stony sides. I started to run along it, as fast as I could, dreading the sight of a figure appearing above.

Soon the gully widened and the sides weren't so high. I slowed to a walk, my breath rasping in my throat. So far, no sign of Gracie. But she couldn't be far behind.

As the gully ended and opened out, I crouched down behind a lump of jagged rock. Ahead were old stone walls and, amongst them, people. It looked like a group of tourists.

Maybe I could hide among them.

I took a deep breath and started forwards, half running, half walking over the scrub. Nobody seemed to notice. Most of them gathered round a woman who appeared to be their guide. A few others were wandering around some ancient ruins.

I glanced back over my shoulder – and almost fell as fear clenched its fist once more.

Gracie was standing on a low rise, not far from where I had emerged from the gully. She was holding her gun but wasn't pointing it at me. Maybe I was out of range, or maybe she wasn't that good a shot. Perhaps she wasn't firing because of the tourists.

I started to run, stumbling over the stony ground. The tourists were my only hope – but they still hadn't seen me.

I scrambled over a low wall and dropped down into a deep chamber on the other side. An elderly couple were staring at the stones and they looked up when I joined them. I smiled at them, but they just frowned. Not surprising really, I must have looked a state.

I took off my hat and wedged it down a crack between two rocks. Bright orange was just a bit conspicuous. I straightened my T-shirt and followed the tour on into the ruins where the guide was pointing to a series of stone slabs.

"And this is believed to have been an altar..." she was explaining, and my heart leapt as I realised she was speaking English.

I wormed my way between them.

There was a track on the far side of the ruins. I guessed that this was the way they had come and how they would leave.

I looked around, but Gracie had vanished.

19
Tourists

The tour guide moved on though the ruins and the tourists followed. I made sure I kept close in amongst them. Her voice droned. This was a temple and that was a house, but it all looked the same to me: rectangular spaces enclosed by crumbling, low stone walls.

I tried my best to slow my breathing and relax – to blend with the group. But I was sure they could all see how on edge I was.

"Time to return to the boat." The tour guide raised her voice so that the stragglers would hear. I breathed a sigh of relief and glanced quickly round. No sign of pursuit.

The tourists drifted back towards the path, leisurely chatting about this and that. I moved with them. They were quite a large group, but I still felt conspicuous.

I kept looking around for Gracie. Was she lying in wait for me somewhere? Or perhaps she had gone to call MEXA for back-up.

"Hi," said a voice beside me. I looked round. A boy had fallen into step alongside and was smiling at me from beneath the rim of his baseball cap. His face was a mass of freckles.

"Hi." I quickened my pace, but he kept level with me.

"I'm Luke. I'm glad we're going back. That was starting to get boring."

I didn't answer and looked back towards the ruins instead. Something moved in the distance and I peered against the glare of the sun, reflected off white limestone. But it wasn't Gracie, or a MEXA agent. It was just a group of monks walking among the rocks and scrub.

"When did you get here?" said Luke. "Were you with the party that arrived last night?"

I nodded. It seemed safest to agree. In an odd way, he reminded me of Isaac, and I felt a weird pang at the thought.

"Well, then," Luke continued. "I guess if you've only just arrived, you've not had a real chance to explore. I could show you around the hotel when we get back if you like."

"Maybe," I said, glancing back over my shoulder. Was I imagining it or were the monks following us?

"What do you make of them, then?" said Luke. He was looking back, too.

"Yeah, weird."

"I didn't know there were monks living on this island." He held up his hand to shield his eyes.

"There's a monastery," I said. "Weren't you listening earlier?" I gave him a broad smile, but inside I was trembling. They were after the key. I reached up and touched it, still safe under my T-shirt.

Luke laughed. "I guess I wasn't. What's your name?"

"Danni."

"Well, Danni, I think I'll show you the swimming pool first. It's got a really good water slide."

I didn't bother to answer him. We rounded a corner and the path dropped down into a rocky cove that formed a natural harbour. The boat was waiting – a typical tourist boat, rows of seats beneath a yellow awning.

I gave Luke the slip as we joined the boat, ducking down round the back of the wheelhouse. Nobody seemed to have noticed me, but I could see Luke walking up and down between the rows of seats, a puzzled expression in his eyes. The throb of the engine changed its tone and the tour guide was helping to untie the ropes.

"Wait there!" called a voice from the shore.

The monks were approaching us along the dusty track. I hadn't realised they'd got so close. Some of the passengers looked round.

"Can I help you?" said the tour guide.

"There's a girl with you, in an orange hat. She's to come with us."

An uneasy silence fell, the tourists watching their guide. She unfastened the final rope. "I don't know who you are, but I think you'd better leave."

"This is our island," the monk said.

"That's as maybe, but I have a duty of care towards my passengers," said the guide. "And anyway. How do I know that you're real monks at all? You could be bandits or pirates."

The monk looked as if he was about to speak, but then he paused and raised both hands.

"All right, we'll go." They started to back away.

And then I saw it: the boat driver tucking a sub-machine

139

gun away in the wheelhouse. So the tour boat was armed. But then, that was hardly a surprise. The seas could be a dangerous place these days; piracy was rife, and a boatload of tourists was easy pickings.

As we pulled away from the shore, I looked back. The monks were standing side by side on the shore, their heads bowed, their hands pressed together in prayer. One of them raised his arm towards me, as if giving a blessing – or a curse. I shivered.

The tour guide walked up the aisle between the seats, counting heads. Then she moved away to talk to some of the passengers. There was a buzz of chatter among them.

I slipped round and took a seat near the back, beside an elderly man with white whiskers who droned on about life before the seas started rising. I smiled as I listened. Much of what he was saying echoed what Robert had told me on our journey to Greenland, and as I listened I tried to imagine Robert there with me. But the empty ache came back with renewed intensity, so instead I tried to focus on the old man's words and imagine a Europe falling apart as the seas came in. I could almost see the coastal cities as the flood waters breached their defences, and the lines of refugees heading for higher ground. And I thought of MEXA, growing in power bit by bit as governments fell.

"Is that boat following us?" the old man asked.

I looked round. Gracie? Or worse? But it seemed to be keeping its distance. The old man shrugged and continued his reminiscences. Nobody else seemed to notice. I pretended to listen to his stories, but all the time I was watching that boat.

The coast of Malta drew closer. I could see the villages, half flooded, water lapping at the walls of the houses. We turned towards the harbour. It was the same harbour we had left that morning, but now it looked so different. All I could see was danger.

I had to get away, but I didn't know how.

MEXA would be watching for me, waiting for me to make a move. They wouldn't be in any hurry. After all, where could I possibly go?

The tour guide was trapped by an elderly couple who clearly hadn't thought much of the day's adventure. She kept nodding and apologising and never noticed me as I slipped ashore behind her.

I started to walk along the jetty, past the small boats. They were bright colours and a few of them had eyes painted on their bows. I couldn't get rid of the feeling that they were watching me.

Maybe I should just run now: sprint for all I was worth and hope I could find somewhere to hide before MEXA could catch me. The tourists were strung out along the harbour side, looking at the boats and stopping to take photographs. I quickened my pace.

Then someone grabbed my arm.

I gasped and spun round.

The old fisherman I had met that morning was looking at me from beneath whiskery eyebrows.

"Danni," he said. "You must come with me, now. I can help you."

"I-" I faltered and looked round.

"Please, Danni. That island you went to – it's dangerous. You should never have gone."

"How do you...?"

"Because I took your parents there the day they died."

"Danni!"

Luke was walking towards me along the harbour side, waving and grinning. The boat that had followed us was just turning into the harbour.

I needed to disappear – and fast – and this man had known my parents. Maybe, just maybe, I could trust him. I didn't feel like I had much choice.

I let the fisherman pull me away. He led me off, into a cafe and out the back. In the cobbled street behind, we started to run.

20
The Refugees

The fisherman led me along back alleys and through narrow, winding streets. Houses rose, towering together overhead as if they were about to topple into one another.

We climbed steadily upwards, slowing to a walk, and several people greeted the fisherman as we passed. It was good to see their smiles.

Behind us I could hear the distant throb of a helicopter.

"You said you knew my parents?" My heart was thumping. There were so many things I wanted to ask him.

"Yes, I knew them." He glanced up at the sky. The beat of the rotors pulsed through the air.

"You said something about their accident. You took them to the island."

He nodded, a slow, thoughtful nod. "I took them to Comino in my boat."

"They were going to the monastery, weren't they? They

were looking for the scrolls." My mind was racing.

The throb of the helicopter was closer now, matching the pounding of my panicking heart.

"We need to get moving," said the fisherman, lengthening his stride.

The houses here were further apart and low walls separated plots of ground with melons in neatly irrigated rows. Prickly pear cacti, all spines and lumps, grew alongside the road.

"They told me it was a diving accident," I said. "So what happened?"

"I took your parents to the island and I waited. They just never came back. But it was another day before their bodies were found in the caves." He gave me a sharp look. "I'm sorry, Danni."

My mouth was dry and my head spinning. My world was turning upside down. My parents had gone there, to that same monastery, looking for the same scrolls. And they had died because of it.

"They were murdered," I whispered. "And it was covered up. I was told it was a diving accident – that they drowned in the caves when they got lost and ran out of air. They..."

He shook his head.

"Did MEXA kill them?"

"MEXA?"

"MEXA. You know. That space agency?"

He looked completely baffled. But then, why not? Most people thought MEXA were just a space agency.

"Why are you helping me?"

"I liked your parents. Your mum made me laugh, always joking, and your dad told such wonderful tales about their adventures. And then they died when I should have been looking after them. I don't want the same thing to happen again."

As he spoke I could almost see my parents, Mum twisting a strand of hair around her finger as she talked, and Dad trying to look serious, his eyes filled with laughter. It was as if they were telling me to trust this man. But then, I'd thought I could trust Gracie, too.

The helicopter was closer now. The fisherman glanced over his shoulder. I paused and started to turn. But his hand was rough on my arm, grabbing me, pulling me down.

I gasped. "But what..."

"Get down." He pushed me into the space between the stone wall at the side of the road and a particularly large prickly pear cactus. The spines scratched my arms and legs. He scrambled in behind me.

And then the helicopter was above us, its down draft blasting dust into my eyes. I tried not to scream as it hovered overhead. Then, slowly, it drifted away.

"Shh, stay here a few moments," he said as the helicopter moved off over the dusty fields, a brown pall following it like smoke.

We scrambled out from our hiding place and continued along the road at a brisk walk, always listening in case the helicopter returned, but it seemed to have moved back towards the town.

Soon the fisherman opened a gate and led me across a field. We walked in silence, dry earth beneath our feet and the sun beating down from above. It was starting to sink towards the horizon, but the heat was just as intense.

He stopped in the far corner of the field where a ruined

building was propped up against the stone wall. There was a metal grille covering a hole in the ground. When he pulled it back I saw steps hewn into the rock. They vanished into darkness.

I looked up at him.

And then I heard the helicopter again, rising up from the town, coming back our way.

"Quick," said the fisherman. "Get down there."

My shoes slipped on the slick stone steps, worn by the passage of many feet. I held out my hands, feeling my way along the rough stone walls.

Behind me, the grille slid back into place and then the helicopter was above us, its rotors pounding through the gloom. It was as if the rock itself was pulsing. I crept on down into the dark and damp.

Behind me the fisherman switched on a torch and a faint pool of light lit the steps in front of me. My own shadow formed a patch of deeper darkness that I stumbled through.

The steps ended and there was an uneven path leading on into the depths of the rock. Up ahead was a glow of light.

I crept forwards. And stopped.

Ahead of me was a cave: small, cramped and full of people. They huddled together in the light of a single lantern, staring at me from frightened eyes.

Then the fisherman pushed past me and their fear evaporated.

"Who are these people?" I asked.

He smiled round at them.

"These people are refugees from the Nile Delta region, forced from their homes by the rising sea."

"But what are they doing here?"

"They're heading to Italy, for a better life."

"But I thought all the European countries had closed their borders."

"Who said they were going there legally?" said the fisherman with a grin. "Why did you think I hid from that helicopter? Come. Meet Fatima. She speaks good English. She will take care of you for now. Tomorrow we will get you off this island and on a plane back home."

A young woman with twinkling eyes and a smile as generous as her hips nodded.

I turned back to the fisherman.

"Did you say they were going to Italy?"

"Yes."

Isaac was in Italy. He was the only person I knew I could really trust.

"Can I go with them?"

"You want to go to Italy with these people?"

"I have a friend in Italy. He can help me. I just have to get there."

The fisherman paused. Fatima smiled at him.

"Of course she can."

"All right. If that's what you want," said the fisherman, shrugging his shoulders.

"Come, child," said Fatima. "We have food. Join us. The boat will be here soon."

"What boat?"

Fatima's smile broadened.

"The boat that will take us to Naples. It will be here as soon as it is dark, and then we can leave this cave and join it."

She held out a paper plate towards me, piled with sweet-scented rice. My mouth watered and I moved across to join her, crouching in the lamplight.

The shadows moved across the cavern walls. I looked around as I scooped the rice into my mouth. The shadows consolidated into lines – strange patterns etched into the rock face by water and time. It reminded me of the writing on the cavern walls in Greenland and I paused, a handful of rice hovering in front of my half-open mouth. Perhaps this was one of the caves the abbot had spoken of, where the last survivors of that ancient civilisation had taken refuge all those millennia ago.

I looked over at the fisherman. He had noticed the look in my eyes and was watching me.

"Is something wrong?" he asked.

"I was just wondering, are these caves very old?"

The fisherman shrugged. "Possibly. All caves are old, aren't they?" He looked round at the walls, then turned his attention back to his food.

I scooped up the last grains with my fingers, then sat with my back against the cave wall, hugging my knees close. Some of the refugees were trying to sleep but I sat, awake, my mind buzzing. It was strange how much my life had changed in a few short days. I remembered the warm smile in Isaac's eyes when he'd handed me my hat on the last day of term: the hat I had lost in Greenland.

But the thought of Greenland reminded me of Gracie and I felt something twist inside me. Had she been planning this all along? Planning to betray me? Why had I ever trusted her? I tried to stop thinking about it, but the hurt wouldn't leave.

A footstep sounded in the passage and another man appeared, burly and sun-browned, face furrowed by the passage of time and ravages of salt and sun. The two men embraced, then the fisherman turned towards us.

"There is no time to waste. Your boat is waiting."

Fatima handed me a scarf and I pulled it up over my head and followed the refugees out into the warmth of the night.

There was no moon in the cloudy sky and it was pitch black outside. We walked in single file with only a lantern up ahead to guide us. I felt the way with my feet and stumbled more than once. I pulled the scarf over my face, glad to feel anonymous.

We picked our way across the fields and then down a narrow cliff track. The boat was bobbing gently below, a darker shadow against the oily black of the sea. Its deck lights were off. The fisherman raised his lantern and waved it slowly back and forth.

A simple signal.

A door opened and a flood of light swamped the deck, to be quenched just as quickly as the door slammed shut

A gruff voice spoke rapidly in Maltese; then I heard a scrape as the gangway was lowered.

"Quickly," said the fisherman. "On board."

The refugees shuffled forwards and I went with them, the fisherman nodding his head as I passed as if to say goodbye and wish me well.

There was metal and wood beneath my feet instead of rock and I felt a mix of excitement and fear as I left solid land behind. The gangway swayed with the swell and creaked against the side of the ship.

"This way," said the voice, and another door opened. Behind it was a hatch, and inside was nothing but darkness.

We pressed forwards and followed the man down into the hold, feet slipping, eyes straining for the slightest light. Fatima was beside me and she put her arm around me, holding me close. We huddled together in the dark. I was glad of her touch, glad of at least one friendly person.

The crewman struck a match and lit a small oil lamp. I saw for the first time that he was armed. A sturdy looking machine gun hung from his belt and he wore strips of bullets over his shoulders like a bandit.

"Right, you lot," he said, his English thick with an accent. "Make yourselves comfortable."

He scrambled back up out of the hold and the door slammed shut above us, bolts sliding home. This was more like a prison than a sanctuary, and a cold sweat broke out over my back.

I looked around. There was a heap of blankets over on one side of the hold and a couple of buckets on the other. From their stink, they clearly served as toilets. I wrinkled my nose as the throb of the engines increased, vibrating through the deck under my feet. The ship began to pitch and roll.

We were on our way.

21
Naples

We spent that night and most of the next day crouching in the darkness of the hold. It was evening before I felt the movement of the ship lessen and heard the rattle of a chain as they dropped the anchor. Everyone looked around nervously. This was it. We had arrived in Naples.

The hatch opened and the crewman was silhouetted against starlight.

"Everyone out," he ordered.

Once on deck I stared out across the oily surface of the sea. We were some distance offshore, but the lights of Naples reflected on the water and made the sky glow.

There was no wind, just the humid heat of night.

"This way."

They were loading us onto a small motor launch, everyone taking it in turns to clamber down a rope ladder onto the rocking deck below.

I pulled the scarf close and shuffled forwards to scramble down with the others.

As we drew closer to land, I could see the flood damage on the low-lying buildings. They were empty, black shadows against the city lights further up the hill. Buildings long abandoned, left for the sea to claim.

We passed over submerged buildings, some only just visible through the murky waters, others breaking the surface with their roofs. Closer in, more buildings jutted from the sea, semi-derelict, their roofs caved in, shutters ripped from their hinges and hanging limp, flapping with the waves.

The boat moved between them, low revs, slipping through the water. Some of the lower-level windows were boarded up and others stared out, black and empty. Waves lapped at salt-rotted frames, the rooms behind them flooded.

The sea was slowly claiming this city. I wondered how long ago these buildings had been abandoned, and how long it would be before they succumbed to the sea completely.

Then in one of the windows a light appeared, swayed back and forth and vanished. We headed towards where it had been and two men appeared in a doorway. The moon was full, and I could just make out their shadowy forms.

Ropes were thrown and secured and we scrambled onto a makeshift jetty.

As soon as the last person had left the boat, the motor launch headed back into the night.

We were not meant to be here. We didn't exist.

We were herded into the dark building, along corridors dripping with damp and decay, and down stone steps. Then we were led along wooden walkways that had been erected so that people could move between the flooded buildings.

I had the feeling that the only people who used these routes were criminals and refugees.

Soon, we came out of an alleyway and there was solid ground beneath my feet. The refugees were herded to one side. Where they were being taken, I could only guess.

I dropped the scarf into a puddle by my feet and fell to the back of the group. Then, just as they were being steered into another boarded-up building, I slipped away.

I ran down empty streets. A couple of turns and I was alone among the abandoned buildings.

A narrow alley brought me to the inhabited part of the city and I stopped at the edge of the shadows. I looked across at streetlights and shop facades – people milling back and forth.

Now what? I had no money and I didn't dare use my fake ID. MEXA would be sure to have a trace on it by now, if Gracie had been working for them. I needed Isaac.

I darted across the road towards the thickest clump of people. Once among them, I pushed my way through and headed along the row of shops. The window displays were brightly lit and cheerful but, behind the shops, dark alleyways stank of rubbish and decay.

The streets were bustling with people, smiling faces staring in shop windows or sitting out in pavement cafes. They seemed to have no worries in the world, as if they were oblivious to the derelict, flooded buildings only a few streets away. A dereliction that would close in on them as the sea encroached.

I was starving and shivering with cold. I stared at a window packed with bread in a wonderful array of shapes, and wondered if I dared steal. As if in warning, I spotted a couple of *carabinieri* strolling past, pristine uniforms and white gun holsters.

They stopped not far from where I was standing, and a third man joined them, stepping out of the shadows. He was dressed in black and I thought I caught a glimpse of a red logo on his breast pocket. I squinted across the road at him. Was it MEXA? I couldn't make it out.

He stepped back into the shadows and vanished from sight.

Of course he was MEXA. He had to be. It made perfect sense that MEXA would have infiltrated the Italian police. And they would be looking for me. I'd told Gracie often enough about Isaac. It was obvious I'd come here looking for him. My hands tensed into fists. How could I be so stupid? If I couldn't even look after myself, how could I possibly hope to help Robert?

It wouldn't be long before they tracked Isaac down.

I had to get there first.

But how was I going to contact him?

The *carabinieri* had doubled back on themselves and were approaching, walking along the opposite side of the road. I moved away from the light.

There was a cafe on the corner of the next street and I paused outside. The smell of freshly ground coffee made my mouth water. There were computer terminals around the walls. At the nearest one, a man was sitting munching a pastry and sipping espresso.

Behind him, on the bar, was a phone.

I stared at it. Maybe, just maybe.

I slipped in through the door.

The waitress hadn't noticed me. Two fat, bald men were flirting with her over at the other side of the bar. I picked it up and dialled Isaac's number. I held my breath. *Please be in.*

Isaac came onto the line, jabbering in Italian.

"Isaac, it's me."

"Danni?" He sounded really surprised. "What on earth? Where are you calling from?"

"I'm in Naples."

"Naples? How..."

"Isaac, I don't have much time." One of the bald men was giving me an odd look. The waitress would spot me in a minute. This was probably her phone I was using.

"Okay, how can I help?"

"I've no money Isaac, and I don't dare use my ID. I think MEXA are following me."

"All right, Danni. You need to come here, to Florence."

"But I've no..."

"Go to the station. I'll pay for your ticket for you. You can get it from any of the machines. Password 'Greenland'. Got it?"

"Greenland. Okay. So when's the next train?"

"Oi!" A shout followed by a burst of rapid Italian.

The waitress was barging her way across the cafe towards me. Her face was red and she was waving her arms around. I dropped the phone back down onto the bar and ran.

I barged past an elderly lady who was half blocking the doorway and burst into the street. Behind, I could hear angry shouts.

I sprinted through the crowds, aiming for the busiest streets and keeping close to the largest groups of people. No one was following. I slowed to a walk. My stomach gnawed inside me.

I stared around. I didn't know this city at all, a confusion of streets and lights.

I had to find the station. And when *was* the next train to Florence? Isaac hadn't got that far.

I kept walking. I only hoped I was walking in the right direction.

22
The Station

I hugged my arms close as I walked past pavement cafes and restaurants. People were sitting out in the evening warmth, wine and chatter amid the city lights. A street entertainer juggled a baton and a crowd gathered round. His face was fixed in a smile, but his eyes were sad. His hat, on the kerb beside him, lay empty.

I pushed my way past. Another time I would have stayed to watch, but for now I had to find the station.

At last I came to a wide piazza. Buses were parked around the edge and straight in front of me was the station building. I hurried towards it.

The outer doors were closed. Old newspaper and other debris had drifted against them. Inside, the station terminal was dark. Maybe the trains didn't run this late.

Was this really where Isaac had meant me to come? He said he would buy my ticket. So there had to be a ticket dispensing machine here somewhere. Didn't there?

I looked back at the piazza and the people milling back and forth between the buses. Two men were walking across the piazza towards me. They were both dressed in black.

I froze. MEXA. But they hadn't seen me. At least, not yet.

I had to get out of sight – and fast.

I pressed my hand against the door. The glass was broken and the lock hung from its fixing. I wasn't the first person to come this way. I pushed it partly open and squeezed through the gap.

Inside, the station was dark and damp. It smelled of decay and stale urine and I wondered who else might be lurking here. Every scuffle and scrape seemed louder, more threatening. I took a deep breath and tried to calm my jarring nerves. There was nobody here. Just pigeons and rats.

I passed by a row of ticket machines. They were dead. None of these machines had dispensed a ticket in a very long time.

But the MEXA agents were still outside. I crept on towards the platforms.

The escalators were still and thick with grime. The further I went, the damper and colder the place became. I could hear the drip drip drip of water in the dark. There was no other sound.

At last I emerged onto the platforms and stared up at the sky. The moonlight was cold and clear. Behind me the sky glowed orange with the city lights.

But the moonlight was reflecting back at me in silver ripples.

For a few moments I stood and stared. And then it dawned on me. I was staring at dark, oily water rippling in the moonlight. I was staring at the sea.

The platforms were still there but, between them, the tracks were flooded.

A shadow moved.

I froze, straining my eyes against the darkness. Who was in here with me? I started inching backwards.

The shadow moved again. And another. There were people down here, creeping towards me in the dark.

I turned and fled.

My footsteps echoed off the damp walls as I pounded back up the stairs and along empty walkways. I had no idea whether I was being followed or not. I didn't care. I had to get out of there fast. There were no trains, no tickets.

Why had Isaac sent me here? Was he leading me into a trap? Was there nobody I could trust?

I burst out of the doors back into the piazza and stood under a streetlight, chest heaving. I searched around for the two men I'd seen earlier, but they had gone; there were just people milling back and forth, queuing beside the bus stops, clambering on board in a shuffling line.

Of course. Buses.

Isaac had never said anything about trains – he just said to go to the station. And then the guilt hit. How could I ever have doubted him?

I walked along the line, looking up at the destinations written above their windscreens. Roma, Torino, Firenze.

Florence. This was it. The passengers were aboard and the driver was filling in some paperwork. He hadn't started the engine yet.

But I didn't have a ticket.

My chest was tight as I looked around. Where would my

ticket be? I didn't have long. The bus was about to leave.

I spotted a man coming out of a shop clutching a newspaper, and I saw the 'T' sign above the door. A *tabernacci*. I slipped inside, hoping to avoid the eye of the proprietor. After all, I wasn't going to buy anything. But he was watching me from narrowed eyes.

There was a machine, tucked away in one corner as if forgotten. It was lit up.

This one was working.

I slid over to it and stared at the screen. I didn't have a clue what any of the writing said. Then I spotted a small union flag icon.

I pressed the screen.

The words appeared in English and I drew a deep breath. There was the option for pre-ordered tickets.

My hands were shaking as I typed in the password and I waited, trembling, as nothing seemed to be happening.

The machine spat out a ticket.

I grabbed it and ran back out into the street.

But I was too late. The bus was revving its engine and the doors were closed.

"No," I screamed as I ran towards it. The driver was shifting it into gear. I waved my arms and ran out into the road, ticket held high for him to see.

He glared at me and then he frowned.

"Please... please..." I gasped although I knew he couldn't hear me.

I thought for a moment he was going to run me down. But then the doors hissed open.

I scrambled aboard and he nodded towards the back. The doors shut behind me and we lurched forwards.

A window seat was free right at the back, and I huddled myself into the corner. I leaned my head against the glass and stared out at the city, trying to get as comfortable as I could.

This was going to be a long night.

"I'm on my way, Isaac," I muttered under my breath.

I really hoped he'd have some answers.

23

Isaac

It was late afternoon of the next day when we finally drove into Florence. I looked out at the tall buildings that lined the river Arno. There was a market bustling with people.

We drove into a broad piazza and my heart jumped as I spotted a familiar figure. I pressed my face close to the window, palms flat against the glass. I could feel my stomach turning somersaults. It was such a relief to see him.

Isaac saw me and flicked his hair back out of his eyes with a toss of his head.

It seemed to take forever for the other passengers to disembark. They all moved so slowly, hoisting down bags and luggage and pausing to thank the driver. I shifted from foot to foot at the back, resisting the urge to shove my way through. But at last I had solid ground beneath my feet and Isaac was in front of me.

He kissed me on both cheeks in true Italian style, then

took hold of my hands.

"Great to see you, Danni. No luggage?"

"No." I was intensely aware of his hands holding mine, and of the moment he let them go.

"And you're all filthy," he said, wrinkling his nose.

I jabbed him with my elbow. "Isaac, you're such a charmer."

He smiled and pulled a small red flower out from under his jacket. "For you."

"A weed, how romantic." I ruffled his hair.

Isaac blushed. "Well, come on. I bet you're hungry."

I nodded. No kidding. I could have eaten an elephant. Twice over.

Isaac had borrowed his brother's moped. I say borrowed, but I suspect he hadn't actually asked. Joe was four years older than us. He had a licence for this thing. There was no way Isaac would.

I scrambled on behind him, hanging on to his waist. He hadn't brought helmets and the wind whipped through my hair as we took off up the road, rattling over the cobbles.

The road led away from the river and soon we were on the outskirts of the city. We headed uphill where fine-looking houses lined the road. Here Isaac stopped.

"Home," he said with a smile, taking off his sunglasses to wipe them on his shirt.

I stared up at the cream-painted walls and blue shutters. Tubs of red geraniums lined the steps that led to the front door.

"Come on, I'll get you some food." Isaac started off up the steps.

"I wouldn't mind a shower," I said as I followed him in through the door.

By the time I'd showered and changed into some clean clothes of Isaac's, he had made a big bowl of pesto pasta. I sat down eagerly, damp strands of hair hanging across my face. This was my first proper meal in days, and it was the best pasta I had ever tasted, with sweet pine nuts and basil.

Isaac sat opposite me.

"Okay," he said. "You'd better tell me what's been going on. I've been trying to contact you. Why didn't you call me back?"

I gave him a sheepish smile. "I'm sorry. I got your message, but then my phone got ruined and I never had a chance."

"So tell me, how did you end up in Naples?"

I ate, and talked between mouthfuls. Isaac sat in silence, listening intently. Only when I paused did he urge me to continue. When I told him about Gracie's betrayal, my voice stated to shake. Isaac reached out and put his hand on my arm.

"It's all right," he said. "I'm here. I won't let you down."

I smiled through my tears. Isaac was the best friend in the world. And it felt so good to be with him now.

Then I told him what the fisherman had said about my parents' death and my voice started to crack.

Isaac opened his eyes wide. He came round the table and put his arms around me, rocking me gently back and forth.

"It's okay," he murmured. "We'll find out the truth, I promise."

I wanted to lose myself in his arms. I reached out to hug him back.

"Hey, Danni."

I blinked and looked up.

Joe stood in the doorway, too much hair gel and a smug

grin. "This is a surprise."

"Go away, Joe," said Isaac, stepping away from me.

"Oh, I'm sorry. Am I disturbing something? Mother never said we were expecting visitors."

I looked across at Isaac, hoping he was as annoyed as I was at Joe's intrusion, but his face didn't betray his thoughts.

Joe opened the fridge door and studied the contents. "Hey Isaac, have you been using my scooter again?"

Isaac didn't answer.

"So how much is it worth, not to tell Dad?"

"Come on, Danni. Let's go to my room."

Joe pulled out a carton of milk. "Nice outfit, Danni," he called after me as I followed Isaac out of the kitchen. "Is the 'boy' look some kind of new trend?"

Isaac muttered something in Italian and ushered me upstairs. Behind, I could hear Joe laughing.

In Isaac's room I climbed onto the bed, tucking my feet underneath me and hugging a cushion. Isaac sat in a chair opposite and leaned forwards intently.

"Do you really think that your parents could have been murdered?"

I nodded.

"But why? And by who?"

"I think they were after those ancient scripts. Whatever it was we found in that cave in Greenland, those scripts show how it should all be fitted together. I think MEXA killed them. I think MEXA killed Kris."

"And you have the key. Can I see it?"

I un-looped the cord from around my neck and handed it to him.

Isaac turned it over and over in his hand.

"Weird. It wasn't red before," I said.

"It wasn't?"

"It was white."

"And it's warm, too; not just from your body heat. It's got its own heat source. Incredible. I've never seen anything like this." He handed it back to me and I tucked it out of sight.

"It's so small, and yet it seems so important."

"And you've no idea what it does?"

I shook my head.

"Remember you asked me to send that email from your account?"

I nodded.

"Well, there was a message for you – from Kris."

"What?" I sat up straight. The cushion I had been clutching fell to the floor.

He nodded. "The email – it's photos of Mars. Photos taken during the Mars Mission."

"Show me."

Isaac spun his chair round and tapped on his keyboard. Kris's email appeared on the screen. It hadn't been sent from her normal account. I swallowed and moved across to read it.

Dear Danni,

These pictures are from the Mars Mission. They show the reason we went there. I've sent them to you because they're monitoring Robert's email. He will know what to do with them. I'll see you soon.

I love you.

Kris.

"And now look at the pictures." One by one, Isaac brought the images up on the screen.

"Is that really Mars?" I said at last, staring at them. "What is that? It looks like..."

"A crashed spaceship?" said Isaac with a grin.

I shook my head. "But this is incredible. And to think that MEXA just happened to..."

"They must have known it was there, just like the abbot said. That's why they picked this landing site. They were looking for the key."

I reached up and touched it, lying warm against my skin.

"Why did Kris take it?" I whispered, half to myself. "She must have known MEXA would come after her."

"Why was Kris there in the first place?" said Isaac.

"She's an astronaut." What was he getting at?

"I've been looking up her records. You know she used to work for NASA?"

"Yes, they have a Mars programme, too."

Isaac chuckled. "Robert must have known that MEXA was on to the contents of the thesis. That's why he asked Lucy to hide it for him, and why he asked Kris to move from NASA to MEXA. He knew they were after the key."

"And this machine. What do you suppose it does? Why's it so important?"

"I'm not sure. Guess it's time for me to do a bit of research." He turned towards his computer and started tapping away at the keys.

I watched him for a while as my eyelids grew heavy. I drifted back to Malta, running over the bare rock and salt pans of Comino. But I was running through glue and then MEXA helicopters were all around me. And the world spun with me and I was underwater, but I didn't have a breathing tank and there was solid rock above. I kicked out in panic and woke.

Isaac was shaking me.

It was dark, streetlights visible through Isaac's open window. Isaac was grinning.

"Danni," he said. "I think I might have found something."

24
Isaac's Plan

"How long have I been asleep?" I stretched and sat up.

"Hours. I've been busy. Come and see."

Isaac dragged a second chair over to his computer and patted the seat.

"What have you found?" I peered at the monitor. He had lots of tabs open. I noticed one of them was Netgabble.

"What do you know about those artefacts that you found in Greenland? The ones that make up this 'machine'?"

"They just looked like lumps of rock to me. The writing was weird, but they just looked like any old rock."

"Made of the same stuff as the key?"

"Yes."

"But it's not rock, is it Danni? Close your eyes and touch it again. What does it feel like?"

I did as he said, rubbing the object between my fingers. Then I opened my eyes and stared at it. Why hadn't I noticed that before?

"It looks like rock but feels like metal. And it's getting hotter."

Isaac nodded.

"And the diagrams at the monastery show how it all fits together. Danni, I think it's some kind of alternative energy machine. And that key you're wearing round your neck is what makes it all work."

His face was flushed, his eyes wide and feverish. I stared at him in silence.

"Your uncle Robert started out working on alternative energy, and then suddenly switched over into archaeology about ten years ago. All because of that old thesis. Only it wasn't just about some old ruins. It was still all about alternative energy."

"So the machine is a power source? And that's what MEXA were after?"

"Yes, and Robert knew it. That's why Kris joined the Mars mission. That's why your parents went to Malta."

I swallowed. Everything my family had done over the past ten years had been about these ancient people and their strange artefacts. It had been their mission. Now, it seemed, it was mine.

And Robert. How much did he really know about my parents' death? What else hadn't he told me? And why had he kept it from me? He must have known I would find out eventually. So many questions I needed to ask. But I had to find him first.

I tightened my fingers around the artefact.

Could Isaac really be right? Could those ancient people have discovered a source of energy that was unknown to us?

"But it's prehistoric," I said with a shake of my head. "They were little more than apes – they weren't even human."

"But yet they drove their chariots between the stars. That's what the abbot said, isn't it?"

"Myth."

"Kris found the key on Mars, Danni. How on earth would it get there without some fairly advanced technology? You saw those pictures. Your 'apes' flew a spaceship to Mars."

Isaac was grinning. A smug sort of grin. He was clearly pleased with his detective work.

"Okay," I said slowly. "Suppose you're right. The broken rock – metal – whatever – fits together to form some sort of power source. Those scripts that Gracie stole from the monastery show how they fit, and I have the key."

"That's why they're after you, Danni."

My stomach squirmed.

"Isaac, there were MEXA agents in Naples. They've got people everywhere and I think they've guessed I'm in Italy. I can't trust anyone except you."

Isaac blushed.

"And they murdered my parents because they went to Comino and saw the scrolls."

"But what I don't get is why did the Proto People send the key all the way to Mars in the first place? Why didn't they want to keep it?" he asked. "That doesn't make sense."

I swallowed. "The monks said mankind wasn't ready. Isaac, there's something wrong here. All those bodies we found in Greenland... I don't know how, but we have to find Robert."

I tried to remember the abbot's exact words. The Creeping

Madness – that's what he had called it. Was this what had destroyed their species?

"I think I know where your uncle is being kept."

"You do? Where?" I leaned forwards.

"I said I *think* I know." Isaac shot me a sideways glance as he returned to his keyboard. "I don't know for certain. But look at these."

He clicked the mouse and a series of windows popped up onto the screen.

"Isaac," I gasped. "Those are MEXA emails. How on earth?"

"Oh, don't ask," said Isaac with a sly smile. "But I'm good, aren't I?"

I couldn't disagree with that.

"Crikey, Isaac. You hacked the MEXA server?"

"Well, not exactly. There was this guy online at Netgabble while you were asleep. I was asking around about MEXA and it turned out they sacked him last week. Check this out."

"That's from Morgan Pew." I leaned forwards for a closer look. Isaac clicked on another message. This one was addressed to Pew, from one of his men.

"Read it," Isaac said.

"'*Returning from dig site – delivering package.*'" I looked up at him. "Package? That'll be all the artefacts they took. It doesn't say anything about Robert, though. They could have killed him, for all we know."

"Ah," said Isaac. "Look at this one."

"'*Dad. Returning to base. Danni has escaped. She has the key. G'.*'"

"And the reply," said Isaac, opening another message. "From Pew."

"'*You should have tried harder. The prisoner will have to tell us where to find her. Maybe we can manage without now that you have the diagrams.*'"

I looked up at him, my heart thumping.

"'Dad'? Pew is Gracie's dad?"

Isaac nodded.

"And the prisoner?"

"Has to be your uncle."

"But it still doesn't say where he is."

Isaac laughed. "That's the easiest part of all. The MEXA headquarters are here in Italy, over in the Euganean Hills. I bet you that's where Robert is being held."

"But you don't know for certain..."

"It's the best lead we have."

"So what are we going to do?" I knew what he was going to say.

"We're going to go there and take a look."

"But they'll never let us in."

Isaac laughed. "Danni, I don't believe you're being so negative. Considering you made your way here from Malta, surely you're not going to be put off by a bit of security."

I grinned at him. "Of course not," I said. "I'm up for anything. Bring it on."

"That's better."

"Do you have a plan?"

"Sort of." Isaac folded down his laptop screen and put it into a rucksack. "We just need to have a little word with my brother."

"Are you kidding? Joe's never going to help us."

Isaac winked at me. "Watch and learn, Danni. Watch and learn."

25

The Road North

Joe took a drink from a carton of orange juice and put it back into the fridge.

"You want me to show you where Mum keeps her car keys?" He tossed back his head and laughed. "What on earth makes you think I'm going to do that, eh, squirt?"

"We could always borrow your moped, but I think it would be easier for us to take Mum's lekkie car."

Joe snorted.

"You're mad, Isaac. You've been spending too much time at that crazy school in England with all those crazy English people." He pulled a comb out of his back pocket and started to run it through his hair.

"I think Mum might be interested in what I found in your jacket pocket."

Joe put his comb away and glared at his brother.

"Of course, if you lend us the car I'll tell you where I've

hidden it."

The two boys stared at one another.

At last Joe sighed. "All right, when do you want it?"

Isaac winked at me. "How about now?"

"Now? It's eight in the evening."

"Yes."

Joe shook his head. "What did I do to be cursed with a brother like you? All right. Meet me in the garage in five."

Isaac steered me back to the bedroom and started shoving clothes into the rucksack along with his laptop.

"See, I told you: watch and learn."

"What was it? How come you're blackmailing your brother?"

Isaac laughed and shouldered the bag. "It's a letter from his college about his lack of attendance. He'll get found out soon enough, but for now I've got a hold over him. Mum and Dad are paying a lot of fees for his course. I don't think they'll be pleased."

Joe was waiting for us in the garage. He unplugged the car from the charging unit. I climbed in and Isaac took the driver's seat.

"Thanks, Joe," said Isaac with a cheery wave of his hand.

Joe grunted as we drove out into the night.

We kept to the main roads and I dozed as the lights of the other road users flashed past in a blur. I shifted position and made myself sleep.

"Nearly there, Danni," said Isaac, and I woke to see the day broken.

We were driving along the edge of the Po Valley in the pale dawn. Below us, I could see a vast expanse of water – the sea slowly flooding this plain. And, jutting out of the smooth water, was a range of jagged hills.

Somewhere in those hills were the MEXA headquarters. Somewhere in those hills was my Uncle Robert. But even if we found him, how were we ever going to get him out?

I touched the stone, feeling its warmth between my fingers. For a moment I wondered if I should give it up in exchange for my uncle, but the abbot's words echoed in my mind and something told me that was a bad idea.

The road dropped down towards an assortment of low buildings and Isaac slowed the car, but didn't stop.

A ferry was creeping over the water towards us, as if it had all the time in the world. It was a fairly makeshift contraption: a large floating raft, drawn by steel cable back and forth between the island hills and the mainland.

But the slipway was blocked by a barrier and a fierce-looking armed guard was standing on duty. Rolls of razor wire ran down to the shore and for some way along it.

"It doesn't look like MEXA care for visitors," Isaac said as he drove on past. I looked back over my shoulder. We were going to have to find another way onto the island.

A few miles further on was a village, a cluster of houses huddled around the encroaching sea. Isaac pulled over among some trees.

"Are you thinking that there might be some boats down there?" I asked.

Isaac nodded. "Come on, let's take a look around."

The village turned out to be smaller than it first appeared because most of the houses were flooded. The whole place seemed deserted, although a line of washing strung between buildings suggested otherwise. But it was the boats, moored alongside one of the semi-submerged buildings, that caught our eye.

"This one looks good," said Isaac.

He was pointing to the only one with an outboard engine. I walked along the jetty for a closer look.

"It's certainly a better option than rowing. Shame about the chain and padlock, though."

Isaac tugged on the chain and sighed.

"Guess we'll have to row then."

I stared out across the wide expanse of water. The hills suddenly looked an awful long way off.

"It's too far."

I looked back at the boats pulled up on the shore, wondering which would be the easiest to row.

But Isaac was moving away from me along the jetty.

"Look, Danni, look at this."

At the far end of the jetty was another boat, moored some distance from the others. But this one didn't have an outboard engine, or oars. This one had a mast.

Isaac was smiling.

"Remember that sailing course my parents sent us on last summer?"

I giggled. "You kept capsizing."

"I did it on purpose."

I ruffled his hair. "No, you didn't."

Isaac blushed. "It made you laugh." He was looking at me with a strange intensity that made me feel all weird inside. I turned away. "Come on," I said, blushing, and clambered on board.

He joined me and started fiddling with the rigging. There was just enough room for the two of us. I steadied the boom.

"You ready for this?" he said.

"Definitely." I loosened the mooring ropes and we pulled away.

I trailed my fingers in the water as the sail billowed on the breeze, and watched the Euganean Hills draw ever nearer. There was a knot in my throat. *Please let me find Robert.*

26
MEXA Headquarters

We dragged the boat through thick mud and hid it as best we could in the long grasses close to the water. I tugged on the cord around my neck. The key was burning into my chest.

Isaac gave me a sideways glance. "You keep fiddling with that thing."

"It's getting hotter."

I wiped my bare feet on the grass to shift as much of the sticky slime as I could, then pulled on my socks and trainers. Now there was thick mud on my hands and I wiped them across the front of my T-shirt, leaving a long grey stripe.

"Eugh."

Isaac laughed. "You've got it on your face, too."

"So have you." I said, wiping a trail across his cheek. He looked rather cute in muddy war paint.

"At least we're camouflaged now," he said, but he'd cleaned it off by the time we left the shore.

We headed up into the hills following a rough track between the trees. It came out on the edge of a road, black tarmac in the midday sunshine.

"This'll be the road that leads to the base," said Isaac.

He started to move forwards, but I reached out and pulled him back.

"No. We'll stay in the trees. Wouldn't want Morgan Pew to come driving past on his way to work."

Isaac nodded. We backed away into the cover of the woods. Just in time. A car swept round the corner with a rush of air and disappeared down the road between the trees.

My heart was thumping. That was close.

It was slow going, pushing our way through scrub and branches. I started to wonder if the road would be a better option, after all. Another car swept past. Best not to risk it.

Then we reached the fence. Suddenly it was right in front of us and we had almost walked into it. I stared up at the rolls of razor wire with a sense of foreboding.

"We're not going to try to climb that are we?" I looked over at Isaac.

"Certainly not. Or cut it. We're going in through the front door." He looked smug.

"What?"

In reply, he led the way along the fence back to the road where two large metal gates blocked our way, ugly looking spikes jutting out along the top.

"Looks pretty impenetrable to me," I said, squinting up at the iron spears.

Isaac moved over to the side of the gate. There was a keypad attached to the concrete post which he stopped to study.

"Are you hacking their security system?" I asked.

He didn't look round. "No."

"Then what are you doing?" I crept up beside him to get a better look.

"Typing in the security code."

"But how?"

Isaac winked at me.

"Someone with a massive grudge against Pew."

It took a couple of seconds to sink in. "Oh, your new friend on Netgabble." I watched as he started to key in the code.

"Damn," he muttered, pulling his hand back from the pad as if it had bitten him.

"What's wrong?"

He didn't answer. Then something moved and I jumped in alarm. The gates had started to swing open.

"Isaac, did you do that?"

"No. Someone else activated it remotely. Quick." He grabbed my hand and pulled me behind him, up to the opening gateway and through, footsteps slapping on the tarmac. We dived into the bushes on the other side, just as a large car swept into view round the bend in the road. It passed us and paused as the gate swung closed. Then it drove off into the trees.

"That was close," I said, my heart thumping. "Well, at least we're in. What now?"

In answer, Isaac opened up his laptop. There was a map on the screen.

"Is that the base?" I asked.

"Yes. These blue symbols are the security cameras."

"Cameras?" I swallowed. I should have known that the security in this place would consist of more than just a fence.

"How do you know that's what they are?"

"It's amazing the things you can find online if you just look hard enough." He swept his hair back out of his eyes and zoomed in on the image.

"But how do you know it's up to date, and what about Robert?" I asked.

"Hmm, yes. Not sure." He turned the screen towards me so that I could see it better. "But I think he might be in here. There seems to be a higher density of security equipment and sensors and cameras and stuff. It seems like the sort of place to keep a prisoner."

I nodded. "Okay, so how do we get there?"

"Follow me and keep close."

The key felt hotter than ever as we followed the road. It was easier going than through scrub and trees, but it was a risk. We were in the open. Exposed. Any moment I expected to see a car driving towards us, but when we did see something it was a series of concrete and glass buildings.

Isaac steered me towards the bushes and we peered out through the leaves.

The stark modern structures looked so very out of place in these ancient hills.

And on the front, illuminated red, was the MEXA logo.

"This is it," I said. "How do we get in?"

"Round the side, there's a service door. We'll have to dodge the cameras."

Isaac opened up his laptop once more and studied the schematics. Then he folded it away.

"Ready, Danni?"

"Not really."

"Then stay close."

We crept forwards to the edge of the shrubbery. In front of us was a broad sweeping lawn. Isaac paused. I could see a camera, mounted on the wall up ahead. It was rotating in a slow arc.

"Now."

He broke cover and started to sprint towards the building. I ran after him, as fast as I could, but I was losing ground. How long did we have? I tried to force my legs faster.

Isaac stopped and flattened himself against the wall. I crashed into it beside him, chest heaving.

"Three... two... one... NOW!"

Again he ran forwards and I darted after him. This time we ducked into a doorway.

"Is this it?"

"Not yet."

He was gone again, running. I felt as if my chest was going to burst. I couldn't keep this up.

Isaac dashed into another doorway, but this door was open. It creaked wide and inside was a long corridor lit with low-level emergency lights.

Isaac pulled me through behind him and eased it shut.

"Did we do it?" I asked. "Did we dodge the cameras?"

"I really hope so."

"But how will we...?"

Isaac looked at me.

"We'll know if we get caught."

I swallowed. "Which way now?"

In answer he started to walk, his footsteps light. My own sounded clumsy and loud in the silence.

At the end of the corridor, Isaac paused and checked his laptop again.

"This way."

We set off to the right: more corridors, all deserted, all lit with the same low-level lights with locked doors to either side. One of the lights was faulty and it flickered and gave off an eerie humming noise. I felt as if it was watching me.

"What do you suppose is down here?" I asked.

"Computer labs, I think," Isaac whispered back.

"It's creepy."

"I know."

"Why isn't anyone around?"

Isaac shrugged. We were approaching another junction and I strained my ears for any sound of movement, other than the echo of our own footsteps. I tried to suppress the growing sense of unease.

"Isaac, is it meant to be this easy? I mean, I know you're good, but..."

Isaac glanced round at me. For a moment I thought I saw a flicker of doubt in his eyes.

"We seem to be able to walk right into this place," I added.

Isaac looked up at a camera mounted on the wall above our heads. Like the others we had passed in here, it didn't appear to be working. "Well it's too late to worry about that now. We're almost there." He quickened his pace.

A moment later he hesitated and held out his hand for me to stop. "Wait."

I waited, heart thumping. He was studying the schematics again, crouching down, laptop on his knee.

"Oh, right," he mumbled to himself. "What are they?"

"What are what?"

He looked up at me. "Symbols on the map. Don't know what they are. But the secure area is just round the corner here." He put the laptop away again and smoothed back his hair. His hand was shaking. "Let's just hope they're nothing serious."

"Come on, then," I said.

In front of us was a wide double door.

Isaac touched the handle and the door swung open. He turned to me in surprise. I squeezed past him into the room beyond. Robert wasn't there. It was just a large sterile-looking lab, not a prison cell at all.

"He's not here, Isaac." I felt like crying. "It's just an empty lab."

But Isaac was walking towards the middle of the lab.

The room wasn't empty. It wasn't empty at all. There was something large in the middle, something large and strange. It looked as if it was made of white rock.

My skin tingled as I looked at it and for a moment I thought I could see a faint purple light arcing over its surface. The whole room prickled with electricity and my head started to swim.

"What is it?" said Isaac.

I recognised it at once – the strange lines scratched into its surface – the ancient writing. It was the artefacts we had found in that cave in Greenland. But they were no longer strewn and scattered and broken.

The whole thing had been reassembled.

I gasped. It looked exactly the same as those pictures in the monastery. As I stared at it, I felt the key heat up further. It really started to burn.

And then I heard a movement behind me and someone came into the room.

I spun round.

"Well, well, well," said Morgan Pew, his voice full of scorn. "I see you decided to accept my little invitation."

27

Captives

Morgan Pew stood in the doorway and smiled, a sickly lopsided smile that turned me cold. Isaac put his hand on my shoulder as armed guards marched into the lab. They lined up behind Pew, guns raised ready, but not actually pointing at us – at least not yet.

I'd come so far. To be caught now, like this, when I was so close to finding Robert...

My eyes started to smart with tears.

No. I mustn't cry.

Then someone else came into the room, someone slight and slim with cool hair and trendy clothes.

Gracie.

I glared at her. She had been my friend – at least, I had thought she had. And all the time she was plotting and scheming.

She walked up to stand in front of Pew. Pew – her father –

the man in charge of MEXA.

"How good of you to come all this way," said Pew. His voice was acid. The skin around his eyes creased with a gloating smile. "I must say you are an extremely resourceful girl, Danni Rushton. Another time, I would be impressed."

I said nothing. I gave him what I hoped was my filthiest look.

Pew smiled back.

"Of course, you know my daughter, Gracie."

Gracie stared at the floor. Good. I hoped she was feeling uncomfortable. After what she had done, I really hoped she felt something.

"But you haven't introduced us to your friend."

Isaac and I exchanged glances. Neither of us answered.

Pew sighed. "Just as well. Maybe it's better that we don't know. It'll make your tragic accident that much more convincing."

For a moment, I caught Gracie looking at me, but she quickly turned away.

"Cow," I muttered under my breath. Was this the same sort of tragic accident as my parents?

Pew turned to Gracie. "Does she have it?"

"Round her neck on a piece of string," Gracie mumbled, still not looking at me.

Pew stepped forwards and held out his hand. I reached up to my chest and touched the key – the key that Kris had given her life for, that she had trusted me with. The key that those ancient people had blasted into space to a distant world for a reason that was lost along with their species. The key that MEXA were so desperate to get their hands on. The key that would make the machine work.

I clasped my fingers around it. It was burning hot.

"No."

"Give it to me," said Pew, and his voice cut through me.

"I think you'd better give it to him," Isaac whispered beside me.

I stood still, taking deep breaths. I looked across at Gracie. How I hated her.

Pew was sneering at me, gloating. I tightened my grip on the key.

"Where's Robert?" I said. "Is he here?"

Pew didn't answer, his hand out, waiting.

"All I want is to find my uncle." My voice was shaking.

The cold look in Pew's eyes hardened.

"I don't think you're in any position to bargain, young lady. Now, give me the key. I don't want to hurt you – yet."

I had no choice. I pulled out the key and stared at it as it lay in my hand, blood red, the lines etched on its surface standing out like dark scratches.

It was over.

I held it out towards Pew.

"I'm sorry, Kris," I whispered.

I had failed. I had lost. And I had betrayed my aunt, my uncle and, worst of all, my parents.

Pew took the key and flinched at its touch.

"What's this?" He held it out, dangling from its cord. "Where's the key Gracie saw in Malta? She said it was white."

"It's changing," was all I managed to whisper.

Pew paused a moment, staring at it, his eyes wild.

"Good. The machine is ready to go and now, thanks to you, we can bring our schedule forward."

He turned towards his people.

"We'll start the first tests at 9 a.m. tomorrow morning. Contact the team and let them know."

All but two of the guards nodded and turned. Gracie followed them to the door without looking in my direction.

"Lock them up. I'll deal with them tomorrow." Pew turned towards me. "Thank you, Danni. Your help has been invaluable."

The guards stepped forwards, guns raised.

Isaac gave my shoulder a squeeze. "Come on, Danni, we'd better do as they say."

"I'll take that, lad," said Pew.

Isaac clutched his bag tight and looked at me. Then he handed it over.

Pew peered inside. "Did you really think it would be that easy to breach our security? Of course, it helps when someone you've just met on Netgabble gives you the key codes. You must have thought you were being so smart, but in truth you're just a child."

I could see the fury in Isaac's eyes, and the pleasure in Pew's as he noted the reaction. Gracie was standing by the door, watching us, waiting for her father. I avoided her gaze and looked back at the machine.

More purple light danced over its surface and I remembered how it had been when we found it, broken apart, surrounded by the bodies of the people who made it.

Then the truth of the abbot's words struck me.

"You mustn't turn it on!" I blurted.

One of the guards prodded me with his gun, but I turned to face Pew.

"You mustn't turn it on," I said, more urgently. "Don't you

see? This is what destroyed the Proto People. This is what caused the Creeping Madness. If you turn it on, we're all going to die."

For a moment Pew looked mildly amused. Then he glared at me.

"Take her away," he snarled to the guards. "I don't want to hear any more of this nonsense."

"It's not nonsense!" I was screaming now. He was going to do this. He would kill us all.

The guard took hold of my arm. His grip was like iron. I struggled but his fingers dug deep and I felt my hand go numb. Tears streamed down my face, partly with the pain and partly with the sense of sheer hopelessness.

"You're going to kill everyone – the whole of mankind," I sobbed. And then I caught the look in his eye. I gasped in shock. "And you know it, too! But you just don't care!"

"Take them away," Pew barked. "And stop their gibbering!"

He gave me a smile that made my skin crawl.

"I guess this is the last time we'll meet."

The other guard took hold of Isaac and they dragged us to the door. Gracie still stood there, watching us, eyes wide. I struggled against the guard's grip.

"You've got to stop him, Gracie!" I screamed as they dragged us out into the corridor. "If he switches it on, we're all going to die!" She turned and looked away.

I kicked out at the guard and he flung me against the far wall, pressing the gun barrel up under my chin. I choked back my sobs.

"I'm not afraid to shoot," he said. "Understand?" I nodded as best I could. They would shoot us down, given half the chance. It would make things so easy for Pew. *They died whilst trying to escape. We didn't know they were children until it was too late. We thought they were common thieves.*

I wasn't going to give him the satisfaction.

Pew and Gracie came out of the lab, securing the door behind them. Pew didn't once look in our direction. It was as if, to him, we were already dead. But I spotted the fearful look in Gracie's eyes as she followed him away down the corridor.

My chest started to tighten. This was all too much. How could it end like this? First my parents, then Kris. And Robert. What had Pew done to Robert?

I had a horrible feeling I already knew.

And Gracie.

Standing there with that man. He'd planned it all along. He must have sent Gracie to the dig site in the first place – to spy on Robert – and then to spy on me.

It was Gracie's betrayal that cut me the most. To think I had trusted her – had called her my friend. And this was how she thanked me.

The guards marched us through a maze of corridors. At the end of one was a heavy metal door.

"You might find your accommodation a bit basic," said the guard. "It's the best we could do at short notice and the penthouse suite is already taken."

His colleague laughed, a tense neurotic laugh. The door swung open.

The room that came into view was small. A single bare bulb hung from the ceiling casting a sterile light onto white walls and grey tiled floor. In the corner was a bucket. And there was a bed, just one, with metal legs and covered by a stained blanket.

Someone was sitting on it. A man with his head bowed and his face in his hands. But even so, I'd know him anywhere.

28

Robert

"Uncle Robert!" I cried as the guard pushed me forwards.

Robert looked up. His hair was matted and his face smeared with grime. He had a large bruise welling under his eye and a bloodstain on his shirt

But even so he smiled as I rushed up to him and threw my arms around him.

"Oh, Uncle Robert, I've found you!"

I couldn't keep it in any longer. Sobs shook my body. I was vaguely aware of Isaac's hand on my shoulder as the door clunked shut behind us. But all that really mattered to me at that moment was Robert.

The only family I had left.

"Danni," he said, his arms tight around me. "Oh, Danni, they got you too." He was almost crushing me, but I didn't want him to stop squeezing.

When we let go of each other, Robert's eyes were sparkling.

"I was frightened you might be dead," I sniffed.

"Well, I'm not," he said softly, wiping a tear from my cheek.

I tugged on his shirt. "I can't believe I've really found you."

The single light bulb started to flicker, casting weird shadows that made Robert's bruises stand out even more.

He smiled. "Even if it means you're locked up in a cell with me at MEXA headquarters?"

I sat down beside him, keeping as close as possible. "Have you been here all this time?"

Robert took hold of my hand. "They brought me straight here from Greenland. They brought all the bodies and the artefacts and all my papers – all my research."

"I know, I saw it. They've got it in a lab. They've put it all together."

Robert nodded slowly. "I thought they might."

Isaac had moved away from us and was inspecting the door. There wasn't a handle and the frame was flush with the wall.

"You won't get it open," said Robert."I've tried."

Isaac didn't stop what he was doing. He bent down and peered through the keyhole.

Robert gave my hand a squeeze. "I was so worried about you, Danni. I didn't know if they had killed you."

"Well, they're going to kill us if we don't escape." I swallowed and looked him in the eye. "Robert, they've got the scrolls from Malta, that the Proto People..."

"Proto People? They were those bodies you found, weren't they?" Isaac interrupted. The door was forgotten. He came over and joined us on the bed, wincing as he sat down.

"The Proto People were a very ancient civilisation, but

not a human one. We're talking about well over a hundred thousand years ago – before our ancestors even left Africa. Back then, before the ice came and the world was as warm as it is now, their civilisation flourished."

"In Greenland?" Isaac stared at him. "They weren't even human?"

"Most definitely not. Danni saw them. Did they look human to you?"

"No," I said, remembering those strange skulls with sloping foreheads and large teeth.

"And the machine?" said Isaac.

"The machine was an energy source."

"I knew it," said Isaac, punching the air. "I knew this was all about energy."

"Pew wants to restart the machine," I said. "We have to stop him. Robert, there isn't much time. He's going to try to start it in the morning!"

Isaac looked at me and frowned. "Surely if it's an energy source though, that's a good thing."

Robert shook his head. "No, Isaac," he said. "That's what I once thought, too, but I was wrong. It's a very bad thing. But luckily he can't start it. He needs the key."

The blood in my veins turned to ice. The key.

Robert saw the look of shame in my eyes.

"Danni?"

"Oh, Robert, I'm sorry." The tears welled up and trickled down my cheeks. I couldn't stop them. I started to shake.

"Danni? What is it? Tell me."

I opened my mouth but all that came out was a croak. Robert and Isaac were staring at me.

"She had the key," Isaac said at last.

Robert's eyes opened wide. The whites formed perfect circles. The colour drained from his cheeks.

"It's true." My words escaped in a large sob. "Kris gave me the key before she died."

Robert's eyes opened wider.

"She had it round her neck all this time," said Isaac.

"But why didn't you say?" The look of horror on Robert's face turned me cold.

"She made me promise. It was the last thing she said to me – "tell no one" – so I kept it secret. I didn't think it would be that important."

"But you know that it is."

"Yes. I saw the pictures at St Publius's. I saw that it was the key."

"That's why they were chasing her," Isaac added.

Robert leaned forwards and placed his hands on my shoulders.

"Danni, this is really important. You have to tell me where the key is now. What did you do with it?"

Sobs shook through me. I had let everyone down, broken my promise to Kris, betrayed everyone I loved.

"He took it, Robert. That horrid man Pew. He took it from me."

"When?"

"Just now. When they caught us in the lab."

"Caught you in the lab?" Robert frowned. "You mean you broke in here?"

I nodded. "Only it turned out to be a trap."

"But why?"

"We were coming to rescue you," said Isaac.

At this, Robert stood up and started to pace back and

forth, punching the fist of one hand into the palm of the other. There was an edge to his voice that I'd never heard before.

"You brought it right to them? Oh, Danni, after everything we've been through." He sounded so despairing, desolate.

"I'm sorry," I sobbed.

"But I still don't understand," said Isaac. "If Pew is going to start the machine then why is it a problem, if it's a source of energy? The world needs clean energy. Even if MEXA are in control."

Robert stopped pacing and drew a deep breath.

"No, Isaac," he said. "Pew must not be allowed to start the machine."

"He's going to start it tomorrow," I said. "He's getting all the team in first thing to get it ready. And Robert, he knows. He knows he's going to kill us all – but he doesn't believe it… or doesn't care. He's mad!"

Robert turned white.

"Are you sure about this?" said Isaac.

"Back in Greenland," I said, my voice barely a whisper, "we found all these bodies piled together around the machine. In Malta, the abbot spoke of a Creeping Madness that destroyed the Proto People's civilisation. Don't you see, Isaac? They switched on their machine, and it killed them all."

Isaac's eyes opened wide. "And is that why they sent the key to Mars – so that no one could ever make it work again?"

"Until now," I said, a shiver running through me.

Robert ran his hands through his hair. "I realised something was wrong back at the dig site. We expected to find the machine, but not to find it surrounded by the dead remains of an entire civilisation. We have to stop Pew switching it on. We have to!"

He turned to the door and started scratching at the edges with his fingers, trying to prise it open.

"It was all there, in my research papers, all the time, references to the cataclysm that destroyed them. It was only after we found all the bodies that I realised what it meant. But then it was too late. And there was no way that MEXA were going to listen to me!" Robert kept on clawing at the door. "I had hoped the key was lost. Pew kept asking me about it, so I knew they had found it and I guessed Kris had taken it – but I hoped she had destroyed it."

"That's what the Mars Mission was all about, wasn't it?" I said. "They were looking for the key. They knew where it was."

Robert nodded.

"See, I was right about that, too," said Isaac.

Robert gave him a weak smile. "When I first discovered the thesis, I talked quite openly about my theories. An energy source that could change the world. It's hardly surprising that MEXA started to take an interest. Just imagine what political clout something like that would give them. After that, it was as much as I could do to stay one step ahead of them. But they knew that the key had been sent to Mars."

"But why didn't the Proto People destroy it?" Isaac asked. "If it had destroyed them?"

Robert shook his head. "Perhaps their religion forbade it. But I'm speculating now. We cannot really know." He struck the door with his fist and swore under his breath.

I buried my head in my hands so they wouldn't see the despair in my heart. Pew was going to turn on the machine and destroy the whole of mankind. And there was nothing we could do to stop him.

29

Escape

We were trapped. We would lose our minds as soon as they switched the machine on and die along with the rest of mankind.

It wasn't a good thought.

Isaac prodded at the keyhole.

"Pity we can't pick the lock."

"Worth a try though, isn't it? It's not a particularly high-tech lock," I said, moving over for a closer look.

"But you don't know how..."

"I've seen it done in films. It can't be that hard. Got any pieces of wire?"

Isaac rummaged in his pockets. Then held out his hand.

"Paperclip?"

"That'll do. Look round for something thin and flat."

He looked around the cell. "There's nothing here."

"There must be something."

"How about this?" said Robert. He yanked at the end of the bed and came over to me, holding a piece of metal in his hand.

"Perfect."

I pushed the paperclip into the lock and gave it a gentle twist. Then I pushed in the second piece of wire and probed around. I could feel the pins. This was going to be easy.

But each time I thought I had it, my hand would slip and the lock mechanism would all fall back into place.

After the fourth attempt, "Sorry."

Robert placed his hand on my shoulder.

"Don't worry. We were all being a bit optimistic there," he said. I leaned my head against his chest, his arm around me. I wanted to cry.

"There's someone outside," whispered Isaac.

I listened. Movement, then a scrape of a key in the lock. I hardly dared breathe. Had they heard us trying to escape? Had they come for us so soon?

The door opened.

I was expecting to see a guard standing there, pointing a gun at us. Or even that evil man Pew.

I wasn't expecting to see Gracie.

She looked straight at me, her eyes meeting mine for the first time since she had a gun pointed at my head.

"Hi," she said.

I moved to take a step towards her, but Robert held me back.

She looked around from one to another. I tried to burn her with my glare.

"What are you doing here, Gracie?"

"I came to let you out. That is – unless you'd rather stay

here?"

"No." I wriggled out of Robert's grip. "This is a trick."

"Danni, he's going to kill you all. I know he's my dad, but you're my friend. I can't let that happen."

I was still glaring at her. "But we're not friends, are we? You were working for MEXA all the time! Did you know they were going to raid the dig?"

Gracie nodded. "Yes. I'm sorry. I called Dad and told him what we'd found. I just didn't expect them to start hurting people. Then Dad told me to stay with you and find out where you went. He hoped it would lead him to the source of your uncle's research. And it did."

"But how did MEXA know what Uncle Robert was...?"

Gracie laughed. "MEXA has always been interested in alternative energy, so your Uncle Robert has always been of interest to my dad." She gave Robert a wonky smile. "He knew you were onto something in Greenland, but you were being so secretive about it. It was almost impossible to find out what you were up to. That's why he sent me."

Robert gave her a sideways glance. "I guess that just made me more of a challenge."

"So MEXA was following Robert all the time?" I asked.

"And your aunt, too, although she made things easy by joining the Mars Mission."

"And my parents?"

"Of course."

I drew in a unsteady breath. "You were in contact with him all the time, weren't you?"

"Yes," she whispered. "You nearly caught me once, that time in the pub."

"That payphone?"

"Yes."

"But MEXA were chasing us – that time they turned up at MI5."

"They'd been following us ever since Iceland, ever since I used my ID to buy our plane tickets."

"But we got away!" I could feel myself shaking.

"The idea was to spook you. They wanted to see where you would run." Her voice dropped to a whisper. "And to make you trust me."

"So why should I trust you now?"

She shook her head. "I can't expect you to. But I can't let you die, either. You need to get away from here. Before they turn it on."

"But Gracie..."

"All that stuff that happened, everything we did – it was scary, but it was great, too. You were a really special friend."

"I..."

She laughed nervously. "I know it sounds weird, but Dad used to talk about your family, a lot. So when you turned up in Greenland, well, it felt as if I already knew you. It felt as if we were already friends."

"But..."

"Go now, Danni. I'll make it look like you broke out. Just get away from here."

I was staring at her. I could feel myself starting to tremble. "What if he finds out it's you..."

"I'm his daughter. He won't hurt me."

I wasn't so sure.

"You could come with us."

She smiled. "I'm really sorry, Danni, about what happened in Malta. I wanted to warn you about Dad, I really did. I should have said, but he's my father. I had to believe him. I won't blame you if you can't forgive me."

I blinked. She really meant it. "On Comino," I said. "You could have shot me, but you didn't."

Gracie nodded.

"You let me get away."

"I should have done more."

I hesitated a moment staring into her eyes then stepped forwards and threw my arms around her. She hugged me back.

"What you said in the lab, about the machine killing everyone. That's why we found all the bodies, isn't it?" she whispered.

I nodded.

"Gracie," Isaac said. "We've got to stop the machine."

She took a step back, looking from one of us to the other.

"It's not just the people nearby who'll be killed," I added. "The effect will spread throughout the whole of mankind. This is the Creeping Madness the abbot spoke of."

"Your dad is crazy. He knows what it'll do and he doesn't care." Isaac placed his hand on my shoulder.

"He's right," I said. "Don't you see it in his eyes?"

This time she nodded. "Yes. He probably thinks he can control it. He thinks he can control everything." Her voice was barely a whisper. "He was going to kill you."

"The Proto People switched the machine on and that's what it did to them. If Pew switches it on, the same thing will happen to our species. Please, Gracie, you have to help us."

"Come with us to the lab, Gracie," Isaac said. "We've

got to find a way to disable the machine, before it destroys everything."

"We're going to do it anyway, with or without you," I added.

She stared at me. "You're mad."

"Nothing new there," said Isaac.

She looked at each of us in turn and bit on her lower lip.

"All right. I'll help you. But follow me."

30
Explosives

Gracie led us along the corridor, keeping to the walls and stopping when we came to a junction. She peered round the corner before waving us on.

"They're all in the village, celebrating the brave new world they think they're about to create," she whispered. "The lab is empty. But we need to dodge the CCTV, and the guards will be doing their rounds. Here."

She stopped outside a door and started to key in a codeword.

"This isn't the lab," I said. "Where have you brought us?"

"It's a storeroom."

The door slid open with a hydraulic hiss. Would Pew's men be there after all, waiting to carry out our execution and then make it look like an accident?

But as the lights flicked on I saw that she was telling the truth – a vast store, floor to ceiling racks of equipment, like giant bookshelves.

Gracie closed the door behind us and hurried to a safe at the far end. She started to spin the combination, pausing from time to time to check a set of numbers she had scrawled on the back of her hand.

"What's in there?" I asked.

"Explosives."

"What?"

"Well, how else are we going to disable the machine?"

"You mean we're going to blow it up?"

"What are MEXA doing with a safe full of explosives?" Isaac asked.

Gracie gave a shrug as the locks clicked home. "God knows. Staging fake terrorist attacks for whatever political agendas they might have, or just left over from blasting out these underground labs. There's all sorts of freaky stuff locked away down here."

"And how come you've got access to this?"

"Dad gets me to run errands for him. I was down here earlier today fetching stuff for them. I had a bit of a nose around."

She pulled out a box and handed it to me. "Here, Danni, you take the detonators."

I stared at them and hardly dared move. How stable were these things?

"Robert, you take the gelignite, and you, what's your name?"

"Isaac."

"Isaac? Nice to meet you. You take this." She handed him a box of wires and cutters and picked up the rest of the explosives, ammonium nitrate and diesel.

This was going to be some big bang. I prayed that Gracie knew what she was doing.

We followed her down empty corridors as fast as we could – as fast as I dared carrying a box of detonators. She steered us past cameras, slowly rotating. I looked up as we ran past. Mistime it slightly, and we would be seen. The thought of that, and what I was carrying, made my heart race.

But then Gracie stopped.

She lifted her finger to her lips and steered us backwards into an alcove. There were no doors off it, just a water dispenser and a bin.

I could hear footsteps.

"A guard?" I whispered and Gracie signalled quiet, with more insistence. A cold chill crept through me. The footsteps were getting closer.

We pressed ourselves into the shadows. Isaac was pushed up against me and Robert moved to the outside of our huddle, protective. This close, I could feel Isaac's heartbeat and hear his breathing. The box of detonators wobbled in my hand.

The footsteps paused. I hardly dared breathe. And then they started to fade and I closed my eyes. All I could feel was Isaac, his breath soft against my neck.

We stayed like that for a few minutes, until at last Gracie spoke.

"He's gone. It's clear." And she led us back out, creeping down corridors and dodging the cameras once more.

Another door, and this time one I recognised.

The lab was empty, as Gracie said it would be. And there was the machine, standing alone in the middle of the room. It was cordoned off, but I ducked under the tape and stared at it close up. One of the ceiling lights had started to flicker and the changing shadows made the strange writing come alive and seem to move. My skin prickled in its presence and my head started to spin, just like when we'd been in this room before.

The machine looked like it had never even been apart. There was just one thing, a small hole in the side at a point where the strange script was more deeply etched. A small hole about the same size as the key that Kris had pressed into my hands, what seemed an eternity ago.

The key was all that was needed to make this thing work.

Robert and Gracie set to work fixing the explosives around the base of the machine. They seemed to know what they were doing and I looked across at Isaac. He joined me, staring up at the structure.

"This is what you found in Greenland?"

I nodded. "It seems such a shame, though, to blow it up."

Gracie stopped building her bomb for a second and looked round at me.

"I know," she said. "But if what you said is true then we have no choice. It has to be destroyed."

She turned back to her work and I watched her, setting explosives, fixing wires. It all looked pretty makeshift. I hoped it would work.

"Let's have those detonators," she said and I handed them over, watching nervously as she fixed them into place. If this lot went up while we were still here... I pushed the thought away.

She took a small remote control unit from the box, pulled out the aerial and pressed a switch. A red LED flashed.

"Armed and ready." She looked round at us. "Come on, let's get ourselves to a safe distance."

We followed her out of the lab and started to run. But we had barely taken ten paces when a shadow moved and a tall figure stepped out of the shadows, to stand in front of us, blocking our way. I skidded to a halt beside Gracie and Isaac bumped into me from behind.

"Well, this is an unwelcome surprise," snarled Pew.

31

The Euganean Hills

"Dad?" said Gracie, a tremor in her voice. "I thought you were in town with the others."

Pew raised one eyebrow. "A good thing I'm not." He glared from one of us to the other. There were a few beads of sweat on his forehead that glinted under the fluorescent lights "How did they get out?"

Gracie took a step forwards.

"I let them out." Her voice was calm.

But Pew's eyes shone with rage.

"What do you think you're playing at, Gracie?" He almost spat the words.

"Stopping you."

For a moment Pew stared at her, then the corners of his mouth lifted into a smile.

"Enough games. The guards will deal with them. And I will deal with you." He gave Gracie a flash of his wolf-like smile and fished into his pocket for his phone.

But before he had a chance to dial, to call the guards, Gracie sprang forwards. She slapped the phone from his hand. It clattered onto the floor tiles and skidded against the wall.

She stood still, cheeks flushed, poised to flee. Pew's face turned red and his eyes glittered with fury.

"I'm not going to let you start the machine," Gracie said. "I'm not going to let you destroy humanity."

"Do you think I don't know what I'm doing?" snarled Pew, his eyes now shot through with red, a tendon jutting on his neck. "Do you think I can't control it? You're just a silly little girl."

"I'm not a child anymore," Gracie said, a slight quiver in her voice. "You don't control me."

"You will do as I tell you. I'm your father. You *will* obey me."

"I will not," said Gracie, firmer now. "Because I see you for what you really are. A petty-minded fool who loves only power. You think this energy machine will let you control the world? It won't. It will destroy the world. And then you'll be nothing."

"You don't know what you're talking about. I'm perfectly capable of handling this machine. It's pathetic people like Mr Quinton here who don't have the guts to transform the world," sneered Pew.

I shrank back from his rage and I could feel Isaac slide his arm around me.

"Well, you won't succeed. Not if I have anything to do with it," said Gracie.

I could see the red LED flashing on the remote as she

raised her hand. Pew spotted it too and his eyes opened wide for the briefest of moments.

"What is that?" he demanded.

"I said I was going to stop you."

She held it high for us all to see.

"Tell me what it is." Pew's voice had risen a note.

Then Gracie glanced round at me. "Danni," she whispered. "Come here."

I slipped out from Isaac's grasp to stand beside her. I tried to look Pew in the eye but the madness and rage in them made me tremble. Then Gracie was pressing something into my hand, almost the same way Kris had done, what seemed like an eternity ago. I felt a chill of foreboding.

"What have you done?" said Pew. "What have you done to the machine?" He took a step towards us. "You are just children. Out of my way."

He barged past Gracie, and I shrank back as he pushed by. Isaac and Robert tried to block his path but he slapped Isaac hard across the side of his face, flinging him against the wall. He strode off down the corridor, heading for the lab.

Gracie held up the remote and the red LED cast a blood-like glow onto her face, flashing on and off.

She turned towards me.

"Get out of here, now," she whispered.

The air seemed to get suddenly colder. Gracie was staring at me, her features were set like chiselled stone.

"That's my car key and pass, get everyone away. Leave me to deal with Dad."

It was the look in her eyes that said it all.

"But you're risking your life for us," I sobbed, the panic

rising in my throat.

And then Robert was there in front of her, blocking her path.

"I should do this," he said. "I found the thing."

"He's my father. I have to do this and you know it."

Robert looked at her and nodded.

"You're a very brave girl, Gracie."

He stepped aside.

Gracie set off after Pew at a run, back towards the lab.

She had gone. I was never going to see her again. I felt so certain that it had to be true. I crumpled to the ground. Tears ran over my cheeks and off my chin. I didn't try to wipe them clear and they dripped onto the floor.

Then someone was beside me.

"Danni." Robert's hand was on my arm, hauling me to my feet. "We have to go. We need to get as far away from here as we can. There'll be time for this later."

Isaac was beside us, one cheek smarting red. He reached out and took hold of my hand. I sucked in a deep breath and started to run.

We sprinted along corridors, stopping and starting, always waiting for the cameras to point the other way. Our footsteps echoed off empty walls. Soon we were in the area of the complex that was lit only by the emergency lights, low level and eerie.

The exit couldn't be far.

And finally the door that opened to the outside.

I dashed out into the cold night air. It was dark round this side of the building and I stared up at a sky pricked with stars. The others stopped too, in the shadow of the building.

"There's a camera," said Isaac. "There's lots."

"We need to find her car."

"The car park's that way." He turned to me. "You'll have to go and fetch it. Let the cameras think you're Gracie."

"Okay."

I stepped out into the orange glow of the streetlights, into full view of the cameras. I could hear my breath going in and out and the pounding of my pulse in my temples. It seemed so loud I thought the whole world must be able to hear it. Gracie had never told me what kind of car she drove.

There were three cars parked round the front of the building. Two of them were large, executive-looking cars. The third was tiny.

"That has to be Gracie's," I muttered to myself. I pressed the key fob and the lights flashed.

I ran over and jumped in. Then I drove back to where Robert and Isaac were waiting in the shadows.

"Quick, you two," I said, "get in."

I moved to climb out but Robert pushed the door back onto me. "No, Danni, you'll have to drive. Nobody will think twice about Gracie driving out. A man at the wheel, however..."

He and Isaac scrambled into the back. "We'll duck low so the guards can't see us."

They huddled down behind me.

My hands were shaking as I steered us towards the gates. When we reached it I stopped and held my breath.

"Just swipe Gracie's pass and we're through," Robert whispered.

I watched as the gates creaked open, turning my face away from a camera that was pointing at me. Any minute they would spot I wasn't Gracie. Any minute the gates would start to shut.

But then they had opened far enough for me to drive through and I pressed my foot down hard on the accelerator.

A hundred metres down the road I stopped the car, the adrenaline still pumping through my veins. I twisted round in my seat, searching out Robert's face in the dim light. "You better drive now, Robert. I'll be no good if it comes to a chase."

After a frantic switching of seats, we drove on into darkness. Through the windows I could see the stars, visible one moment and then hidden by branches and leaves.

The moonlight turned the tarmac grey, but the forest to either side was pitch black. Robert switched off the headlights. We would see any cars by their lights long before they reached us.

"We must be near where we left out boat," said Isaac after a while.

We pulled over by the side of the road and I climbed out to stand in the moonlight. The road swept round in a wide curve, and ahead of us was water.

We stood, staring out. The newly encroached sea, silver ripples beneath a star-strewn sky. And in the distance, a glow of light.

"Is that the ferry?" asked Isaac. His voice seemed loud against the silence of the night.

I opened my mouth to speak.

A flash.

I blinked and stepped back and a few seconds later the ground beneath us shook and the trees swayed back and forth in a rush of wind. Behind the trees the sky glowed red as a plume of flame and orange glowing smoke rose ever higher.

It took a couple of minutes for it to sink in, and then I realised that I could be looking at Gracie's epitaph.

My legs folded.

I sat by the side of that road staring up at the flames, and Isaac sat with me and took hold of my hand.

The tears were back, streaming down my face. But I didn't sob or weep. I just sat and the tears kept coming.

Robert was beside me.

"It's all right, Danni," he said. "We're safe now."

Then his arms were around me, holding me tight.

32

The Graveyard

I huddled beneath my umbrella by the side of Kris's grave and looked down. The coffin was still visible beneath the scattered dirt and flowers. The mourners were dispersing now and the undertakers waited in the background. When we had gone they would fill in this hole.

I didn't want to go. Not yet.

Isaac joined me in the rain-smeared graveyard and his hand slid into mine. The clasp of his palm was warm.

"Time to go, Danni," he said.

I nodded and let him lead me round to the front of the church. Robert was waiting for us with the vicar, and a woman.

I stopped in my tracks.

"What is it?" Isaac whispered.

I tipped my head close to him. "It's Lucy."

Robert smiled when he saw us. "Ah, there you are, Danni.

Look who's here."

"I gather you found what you needed in Cambridge?" said Lucy. There was a smile in her eyes.

I blushed. "Yes. We did."

"That's a lovely hat."

"Thanks. Isaac gave it to me."

"It's a trilby, isn't it?"

I nodded. It really was gorgeous – green and gold check with a black silk band. I wore it everywhere.

Lucy took hold of Robert's hand. I looked at the ground and shuffled my feet.

"Robert here owes you his life," said Lucy. "And I owe you my thanks. You're a very brave girl."

I swallowed. "Was it totally destroyed?" I asked.

"The machine?" said Lucy. "As far as we know."

"And..." I couldn't finish the sentence. Isaac gave my hand a squeeze.

"I'm sorry, Danni." Robert put his arm around my shoulders. "We don't know. Gracie and Pew have disappeared. MEXA are claiming that the building was destroyed by an electrical fire."

"Is she dead?"

"We don't know. There are no reports of any casualties, so who knows. Maybe she got away."

I really hoped he was right.

"Gracie did a very brave thing, you know."

I nodded. "Pew had Kris murdered, didn't he? "

"I believe so," said Robert.

"Did he murder my parents?"

Robert sighed and shook his head. "Perhaps. The police have reopened the case. There's been some sort of cover-up."

"It was Pew. It has to be."

Lucy placed her hand on my arm. There were tears in her eyes. "They're concentrating their investigation on that monastery. It seems more likely that it was the monks."

"Monks?"

Lucy looked round at Robert and he gave a quick nod of his head. She rubbed her hand up and down my arm.

"This order of monks was guarding a great secret. I imagine that they thought killing to protect it entirely justified."

"I still think it was Pew," I said.

"It couldn't have been Pew," said Isaac, wiping the rain from his eyes. "Think about it. You led MEXA to those scrolls. They didn't know about them before. So it had to be the monks."

Lucy took her hand away.

"They will find who did it, Danni. They won't get away with murder."

Robert glanced up at the sky. The rain was coming down heavier and the village was shrouded in mist. "We'd better be getting home."

I blinked back my tears and squared my shoulders. Robert and Lucy followed the other mourners back up the lane towards the village. But I lingered in the rain. Isaac waited with me.

"Look at them all," he said. "They've no idea how close they came. They'll never know that we saved them."

I looked round at him.

"It was Gracie who saved them," I said. "Gracie saved everyone."

about the author

Kate Kelly was born in Edinburgh and spent most of her childhood in Devon. After studying Geology and Oceanography at university, she began a career as a marine scientist. Since then, Kate's job has taken her to the Arctic, where she has seen ice caps up close. Her scientific background influences a lot of her writing, and has helped shape the watery world of *Red Rock*.

In her spare time, Kate enjoys archaeology, kayaking, and SCUBA diving. She's even dived in the Comino Caves, mentioned in this book. Kate lives in Weymouth with her two cats, two daughters, and one husband.

For more exciting books from brilliant authors, follow the fox!
www.curious-fox.com